The Army of Orphans:

The Beginning

F. B. Veneziano

THE ARMY OF ORPHANS: The Beginning

This book or any portion thereof may not be reproduced or used in any manner whatsoever without express written permission of the author, except for the use of brief quotations in a book review.

This is a work of fiction. Names, characters, businesses, places, events, governments, and incidents are either the products of the author's imagination or used in a fictitious manner. Any resemblance to actual persons, living or dead, or actual events, is purely coincidental.

PFC Publishing
ISBN: 978-0692779293

For my husband, Paul,

My beautiful daughter, Cassondra,

and

My best friend, Stevie.

*Your encouragement and love kept me going.
This book would never have happened without
you.*

Thank You

*To my editor, Vicki Adang
who patiently helps me with my overuse of the
dreaded comma!*

CONTENTS

The Army of Orphans

The Beginning

Part I

"Step with care and great tact,

and remember that life's

a great balancing act."

Dr. Seuss

CHAPTER 1

The Way It Was

Life for the Krisko family was happy. We lived in a small house in Pervaiske, Ekrunia. Papa used to tell us stories about how Ekrunia was once part of Ukraine and that there had been a revolution back in 2015, about thirty years ago. The destruction was still visible around the city. To us, they were just stories. The revolution had ended before we were born.

Our house was modest but comfortable, warm and full of fun and laughter.

Yana, my mother, stayed at home to care for us. Irina, my sister, was seven years old, I was six years old, and my brother, Anton, the baby, had just had his first birthday.

Mama was a fantastic cook. She kept a garden in the back, as most of the neighbors did. It took up the entire yard. In summer, she used fresh ingredients from the garden to make her soups, stews, and pies. What we didn't use, she preserved for winter. We stored the canned goods in the cellar along with the grown potatoes.

After school, Irina and I would sometimes help

weed the garden, and Mama would reward us with fresh strawberries and cream, even though she knew we had eaten half of them out in the yard!

Papa worked in the coal mines. It was hard, dirty work, but Papa always said *a man should never be too proud or lazy to work. Providing a good life for his family is the most important thing a man can do.*

We looked forward to Papa coming home every night after work. No matter how tired he was, he would always do something with us while Mama finished fixing supper. We would practice our moves with a football or play cards. Sometimes Papa would wrestle us down and tickle us until we were out of breath from laughing so much. Anton was just a baby, but he would sit in his high chair and giggle at us as if he were part of the fun. In the winter, we would ice skate. We didn't get a lot of snow, but it was freezing. Every day was fun.

***

It was an ordinary Tuesday. Irina and I were at school. My class and I were sitting at our desks practicing our writing. I was pretty good at writing. Mrs. Lipka, my teacher, was walking around the room looking over shoulders and patting backs when she liked what she saw.

There was a knock on the classroom door. Mrs. Lipka walked to the front of the room and opened the door. Two policemen stepped into the classroom.

We all began to whisper, giggle, and ask one another why we thought they were there.

"Back to work!" Mrs. Lipka snapped and went back to listening to what the policemen had to say.

As they spoke to her, she got a strange look on her face, covered her mouth with her hands, and turned her back to us. She nodded to the two men and then turned to face the class again.

She cleared her throat. "Alex Krisko, please go with these officers. They need to take you to the office."

My heart began to pound, and my stomach was suddenly tied in knots.

I stood up slowly and went with the two policemen. They were nice and spoke softly to me as we walked down the hall, small talk…"Do you play sports? Are you doing well in school?"

Even though they were nice, it didn't help with the feeling in my stomach. I tried to think of anything that I could have done wrong in the past few days–nothing.

3

When we walked into the office, my dread increased. Something was truly wrong. Something my six-year-old mind couldn't figure out. I could hear Irina crying in the other room. The school nurse came over, took my hand and led me in that direction.

"Come," she said.

I looked up at the policemen; they looked away as though they didn't want to be part of what was about to happen.

"What's wrong? Is Irina hurt? Why is she crying so hard?" I kept asking questions without waiting for anyone to answer.

I walked into the next room. Irina looked up and ran to me. Sobbing, she took my hands in hers.

"Alex, oh Alex, it's Mama! They're saying she had a bad accident!"

***

The policemen drove us home, and when we walked inside, we found Mrs. Babich there with Anton.

Mrs. Babich was a sweet older lady who lived next door. I once heard Mama say that her husband left one day to go to work and never came home. He just abandoned her. They never had children, and she was all alone. She was like a surrogate grandmother and would watch us whenever Mama needed her to. Today was one of those days.

Mama went to the market every Tuesday to shop for us, and she would pick up anything Mrs. Babich needed as well. In return Mrs. Babich watched Anton. He liked her and was always happy to be with her. But that day Anton was crying loudly. It was as if he knew something was very wrong, even though he was too young to understand what was going on around him.

Irina ran through the house calling for Papa.

"He's not here, *moja doroha* (my darling). The police needed him," said Mrs. Babich.

"Why? What's happening? I don't understand what's happening! Is Mama hurt bad?" I yelled.

She looked so sad. She had tears running down her cheeks. Anton had stopped crying, so she put him in his playpen.

"Come, *dorohi* (darlings)." She sat on the sofa, wiped her tears, and motioned for us to sit on either side of her. She placed an arm around each of us.

"Your Papa will be here soon," she said gently.

"He will explain everything to you. Be strong, *dorohi*, be strong."

"Is Mama dead?" Irina was weeping. "Tell me, please, is she?" Mrs. Babich lowered her head. We knew the answer.

We sat there for a long time, leaning on her, crying as she tried to comfort us.

Then the door opened, and Papa walked in. We ran to him, but he just pushed past us and walked into the kitchen. It was as though he didn't know we were there. He opened a cabinet door, took a bottle off of the top shelf, and poured a tall glass of the clear liquid. Papa took the glass and the bottle, walked over to the table, and sat down.

Mrs. Babich sat next to him.

"She was driving to the market, just as she did every week," said Papa. He was talking more to himself than anyone else.

"If she had left five minutes earlier or later, the truck that hit her wouldn't have been there at the same time she was. Five minutes either way and she would be alive. How could they both arrive at the intersection the exact moment it would take to cause the crash? How is it such a thing could be orchestrated so perfectly and by whom, what power, why?"

Looking concerned, Mrs. Babich reached over and placed a hand on his arm. She very quietly said, "Igor, drinking is not going to help. The children need you now."

Papa seemed to explode! He jumped up and threw the glass. It hit the wall and shattered, spraying its contents everywhere.

"You have no right to preach to me, old woman! Leave my house!"

She looked as though he had slapped her in the face. She stood, slowly, and tried to speak.

"Now, you bitch! Or I will pick you up and throw you out!"

She turned to us and sadly said, "Come over or call if you need me." And she left.

"Go to bed, and take Anton with you," Papa snapped. He reached for another glass and proceeded to fill it up.

Irina and I had never seen Papa like this. He seemed like a stranger, a scary, mean stranger.

That was the first time we saw Papa take a drink. It was also the last time we ever saw him truly sober.

CHAPTER 2

Eight Years Later

Paul Orlik walked home from school with us every afternoon. Paul was Irina's boyfriend. She thought he was the most remarkable boy alive!

Granted, he was the best football (some call it soccer) and ice hockey player in school, and the girls did seem to like the combination of his sandy blonde hair and blue eyes, but most remarkable? OK, he was a pretty good guy, and he was crazy about my sister.

He lived two doors down on the other side of Mrs. Babich's house. He was one of ten children. The family was very poor. His parents were good people, but it took all their time just to survive. Affection and support came somewhere down the list–after food and shelter. At seventeen, he was free to do whatever, whenever. But in spite of all that freedom, neither he nor his sisters and brothers had ever given their parents the slightest problem.

Irina, Anton, and Paul were waiting by the tree on the side of the school where we met up every afternoon.

"Hurry up, Alex. We've been waiting here forever!" yelled Irina. They started walking.

"Hey, guys," I said when I caught up. "How's it going?"

"I was just trying to convince your sister to come to the bonfire with me tonight. We hardly ever go anywhere, and all our friends are gonna be there."

"Paul, please, you know it's not possible, Papa will never let me go. Besides, it's going to be below freezing. We'll turn to ice!"

"Hello–bonfire? Fire, heat?" Irina glared at me as if daring me to say another word.

"Then I'll go and ask him myself, it's about time he found out about us anyway," said Paul.

"*No!* You know how he is since Mama died. He's mean and hateful! He'll not only punish me for being with you behind his back, but he'll take it out on Alex and Anton as well!"

She was right; he would.

Irina had to grow up fast after Mama died. Papa treated her like a chattel. As the oldest and only girl, she had to take over running the house, cleaning, cooking, doing the laundry, all while still keeping up her grades. (Papa demanded we get good grades, the only thing he did right.) Taking over Mama's job was a lot to expect from someone so young. Somehow Irina managed to grow into it, in spite of the abuse.

Now at sixteen, not only had she taken on her mother's job, she had taken on her beautiful looks as well. Irina was of medium height and slender with light brown hair that flowed down to her waist, just like Mama. Her brown eyes were framed by thick, long lashes, just like Mamas. But unlike Mama, whose eyes had been happy and loving, Irina's eyes possessed mostly fear and sadness.

"One day I'll take you away from this. Once we're married he won't be able to hurt you ever again, I promise." Paul smiled and kissed her gently.

"Oh, yuk!" Anton yelled.

"Hey, what are you looking at!" laughed Paul. "I'll show you what happens when you snoop on your sister!"

Paul pretended to grab Anton, who screamed in delight, broke away, and ran towards home with Paul right behind him.

"I'm gonna go to the bookstore today. They got

in a new issue of Spiderman. I've been waiting weeks for it to come in!" I told Irina. I did my little happy dance around her.

Every day just before Papa got home I would go to my room, out of sight. Mostly to avoid being at the mercy of Papa's always sour mood and to read my beloved comic books.

I loved reading about heroes who made things better for people. My favorite hero was Spiderman. He learned early on that with great power comes great responsibility. Spidey vowed to use his powers to help people. I dreamed of having powers to help Irina and Anton, to protect them from Papa.

"I can't believe how much you love Spiderman comics. Where'd you get the money?" asked Irina.

"Mrs. Babich paid me in advance to do some yard work for her," I said.

"Good for you!" she said as she ran off to catch up with Paul and Anton.

They were all giggling and darting behind trees and bushes. I followed behind, getting a kick out of watching them.

When they reached Paul's house, they stopped abruptly. I walked up beside them and saw Papa's car parked in the driveway.

Anton looked up at Irina, a terrified look on his face.

"Irina, why is Papa's car home?"

"I don't know, Anton."

"I'll come with you," said Paul.

"Thank you, Paul. We'll be OK. If something is wrong, having you, there will make it worse."

"But…"

"Please, just go inside. I'll handle it," Irina said firmly.

"We're good, Paul," I said casually, but I had a feeling of dread in my stomach.

Paul knew better than to argue anymore. He kissed Irina on the cheek and said, "Be careful." Then he looked at me and said, "If it gets bad, come to my house."

I smiled and nodded.

As we walked past Mrs. Babich's house, the scent of lilacs drifted up. There were two bushes, one on either side of the small porch. Any other day, Irina would have asked permission to pick some of the fragrant purple blossoms for the kitchen table. But today, it was the furthest thought from her mind.

"Why would Papa be home so early?" asked Anton.

"I don't know, but stay behind me when we walk in and don't say a word," I said.

Irina stopped walking.

"No, stay behind me," said Irina. "Alex is going to the bookstore."

"I can't go now," I protested.

"Come on, Alex. It's Papa. They probably sent him home for drinking on the job. He's in there right now snoring up a storm. I can guarantee it."

That did make sense, and I really, really wanted that comic. If I ran, I could be back in fifteen minutes. In hindsight, it didn't take much convincing.

"OK, I'll be right back."

The front door was partially open. Anton stayed behind Irina, partly because she told him to and partly because he was nervous. He had learned early in his short life that it didn't take much to set Papa off. It was best not to wake him. I watched as they both slipped off their shoes at the door and went inside.

***

I ran all the way to the comic store. I was so excited to get my "new" used book. Mr. Brodsky, who ran the store, was always kind enough to give me first crack at buying the Spiderman comic books before he put them out for sale.

I was nearly home when I saw Mrs. Babich, who had stepped outside her door.

"Alex," she called, "he's at it early today, throwing things and such. I heard the crashing over there. Has something happened?"

"I don't know–I just got here." The excitement I felt quickly turned to dread.

Just then, we heard Irina scream. Papa was yelling. I immediately ran toward the house.

When I opened the door, my heart sank. Broken glass was all over the rug; there were dents on the walls where Papa had thrown vases and knick-knacks.

"Irina! Where are you?" I called, trying to swallow the lump in my throat. *Why didn't I come home with her? Why did I have to go to the bookstore?*

When Anton heard my voice, he came out of his room and into the hall.

"He went crazy, screaming at her! I'm sorry, Alex, I should have helped, but I was too scared to come out of my room!" His face had such a guilty look, and he was shaking uncontrollably.

"It was up to me to be here, not you," I told him.

We walked to the kitchen. More broken glass. The plants that Irina kept on the sill above the sink were thrown across the room. Broken planters and dirt were all over the floor, alongside the ruins of ivy and philodendrons.

"Where is she?" Anton whispered.

Then we heard another scream. It was coming from out back, in the garden.

"Irina!"

I ran out in time to see Irina land face down in the dirt, sobbing. Papa was swaying above her, fists clenched.

"Defy me again! Go on!" he kept shouting in his drunken slur.

"Stop! Leave her alone! You're gonna kill her!" I yelled.

Anton, who had followed me outside, tried to run toward her, but I grabbed him and yelled for him to go back to his room. He fought me. At that moment, his only thought was to help his beloved sister.

Just then, Papa turned and looked at us, his eyes full of fury, and his jaw tight.

"Irina, run!" I shouted.

As Irina made it out the garden gate, I grabbed Anton, and we ran through the house and out the front door.

As we got to Mrs. Babich's house, we could hear police sirens in the distance.

"I had to call," she said. "I thought he would kill her!" She was wringing her hands nervously.

Paul tried to support Irina as she limped over to us, followed by Mrs. Orlik, his mother. Blood covered her face, and she was holding her side. Although she was still sobbing, she managed to ask if Anton and I were safe. I reassured her as best I could. I felt like a real creep. I should have been there to help her, and she was worried about me.

"Paul, could you take her to the hospital?" I asked.

"I'll drive them," said Mrs. Orlik.

"Then I'm going to take her home with me," said Paul. "There's no way she's going back there!"

A few minutes later, the police arrived. Two of them came over to the crowd of neighbors mingling around.

"Who made the call?"

Mrs. Babich spoke. "I called. I was afraid for the children. Mr. Krisko is drunk, and it was so loud over there. Then we heard Irina screaming–"

One of them looked at Anton and me.

"Are these the children?"

"Yes, we are," I answered quickly. "I'm Alex Krisko, and this is my brother, Anton."

"Their sister, Irina, went with the neighbor to the hospital," said Mrs. Babich.

The police officer looked at me and asked, "What happened, son?"

I told him everything that happened since I came home, how Papa was angrier than usual, and how he had gone after Irina. Anton just stood there, not saying a word.

"Where is he now?" asked one of the officers.

"In the house, I think."

"Is he alone?"

"Yes."

"Does he have any weapons?"

"He has a rifle for hunting," I answered. "But it's in the closet where he keeps it."

As the two police officers went next door to see my father, a woman walked over to us. She said she was from the Government Division of Child Protection.

"Are you the woman who called about the children being in danger?" she asked.

"Yes, my name is Marina Babich."

"May we speak over there?" She placed her hand on Mrs. Babich's arm and led her closer to the front porch.

She was still talking to Mrs. Babich and writing notes on a small pad of paper when the two officers came out of the house with Papa in handcuffs. He wasn't cooperating, so one of the officers slammed him into the police car. He opened the door and shoved Papa into the back seat, hitting his head on the roof as he did so. I was relieved to see him in custody. *You deserve more than a little bump on the head,* I thought.

The other officer went over to the child protection lady and said something to her. She came back to where we were standing.

"Where's Papa going?" asked Anton.

"I think he's going to jail," I answered.

"Yes, it seems that he is," said the lady. "I'm afraid I'll have to take you boys to a foster home until this is sorted out."

"What's a foster home?" asked Anton.

"It's a place for you to stay until you can come back to your own home. You'll be safe there."

He began shaking again. I put my arm around his shoulder.

"But, I have a home. I want to stay here with Alex. He's my–"

The lady interrupted him. "Brother, I know. He's coming with you. It'll be fine."

"Can't we just stay with Mrs. Babich?" I asked. The quivering in my stomach had made its way into my voice, no matter how I tried to control it. I didn't want Anton to know, but I was just as frightened as he was.

"Yes," said Mrs. Babich. "They can stay here with me."

I felt hopeful, but not for very long.

"I'm sorry. This situation is a state matter now. They'll have to go to a home that's been approved by the state, and you aren't on the approved list."

"Then I'll get approved. What do I have to do?"

"It takes weeks to get approved as a caregiver, and…" The lady paused, and her face turned red. "There are age requirements that you would have to meet," she said.

"You mean I'm too old," Mrs. Babich said sadly.

The lady avoided eye contact. "I'm sorry," she said.

"What about Irina?" I asked.

"As soon as I get you two settled in, I'll be going to the hospital to check on her."

She turned to Mrs. Babich. "I'll be taking the boys next door to gather a few things, and then we'll be going. The police will be coming back to get your statement."

Mrs. Babich nodded sadly and put her arms around us.

"I will see you soon, *dorohi*. Take care of each other. That's what your mother would have wanted.

CHAPTER 3

The Foster Home

We had never packed before and weren't sure what to take. We had no idea how long we would be gone. I helped Anton, and then packed my clothes and my comics. I felt like I was sleepwalking, going through the motions but not honestly believing it was happening. I kept praying to wake up. The child protection lady came into the bedroom to see how we were doing.

"Did you pack your toothbrushes and underwear?" she asked.

"No, ma'am, we didn't get our toothbrushes. I'll get them," I answered.

"First, come and sit for a minute, both of you…here on the bed."

Anton and I sat down on his bed, not knowing what was coming next. The lady sat on mine.

It was the first time I took a good look at her. She wasn't very old, not what you would expect from a government lady. She looked nicer than she sounded when she spoke to us outside.

"First of all, I don't think of myself as a ma'am.

Call me Anna, OK?"

"Sure," I answered. Anton nodded.

"I phoned the hospital. Judging from the preliminary examination, Irina will be fine, but she'll have to stay in the hospital for a while."

"How long a while?" I asked.

"A few days, at least. Irina has lots of bruising," she answered. "She also needs stitches over her eye, and she has at least one cracked rib. They're giving her a full exam now. As I said earlier, I'll be going over to the hospital after I get you boys settled in at the foster home."

Her face softened, and she smiled gently. "I know this is very hard on both of you," she looked directly at Anton, "and a little frightening."

He looked down at his hands; he was fighting the tears welling up in his eyes.

"But you'll be safe from your father."

I'll be safe? Where was I when Irina needed to be safe?

"He needs help if you're ever going be a real family again. Has he always been like this?"

"Yes," my brother answered quickly.

24

I had never thought about it before. For Anton, that was the absolute truth. He was so young when Mama died, and Papa started drinking. He never knew the Papa that Irina and I had known.

"Our mother was killed in a car accident when he was only a year old. Papa was very different before that. He was a good, kind man, and a great father." My voice trailed off as memories of my past came flooding back.

Suddenly I felt tears welling up in my own eyes. It was a very distant memory, one I had nearly lost; Papa coming in after work and kissing Mama, then turning to us and growling like a monster while he chased us, then tickling us until we were all laughing so hard we lost our breath!

Happy, loving times.

Family times.

Lost times.

Suddenly the sadness seemed to overwhelm me. I felt like I was drowning. I couldn't breathe.

Anna saw what was happening. "Enough talk." She crossed the room and put her hand on my shoulder. "Time to go. You had better get your toothbrushes."

Struggling to keep my emotions under control, I walked to the bathroom, grabbed our toothbrushes, and went back to my room. We finished packing and walked to the car.

As we pulled away, I wondered how long it would be before we would see our home again.

***

The ride to the foster home was quiet. Anton and I sat silently in the back seat. As we pulled up to the house that would be our home for a time, he reached over and took my hand.

It was an ordinary house, a lot like ours, small with blistered white paint. The front door was a peeling green color with the white showing from underneath.

We got out of the car and took our belongings up to the front porch. Anton held on so tightly that my fingers were going numb.

When we got to the door, he looked up at me. I had never seen so much fear in his eyes, not even when Papa was in one of his worst moods. I tried to smile at him and gave him a wink. He gave me a weak smile in return.

Anna knocked. A pleasant looking woman answered. She was a little older than Anna, with dark, brown eyes and brown hair tied up in a bun. She was wearing a dress and an apron that had stains from food and flour. A baby who looked to be about a year old was on her hip.

"Hello, Anna. Please, come in," she said.

We removed our shoes and entered the house.

"Boys," said Anna, "I would like you to meet Sophia Kozel. She'll be taking care of you for a while."

"How do you do, Mrs. Kozel?" Anton and I stumbled over one another's words.

"You may call me Sophia."

That was the second time in one day that adults had permitted us to address them by their first names.

Papa would have been very displeased. He felt it was disrespectful for children to address their elders by anything other their surname unless it was "sir," "madam," or "ma'am."

"We'll do our best. We don't usually get foster children as old as you boys. Normally we care for little ones, like Tanya here." She bounced Tanya up and down on her hip. The baby smiled.

"And we are very grateful. There isn't room anywhere else. Our only other choice would have been the prison," said Anna.

"Prison?" I repeated. My head started to reel. My heart began pounding so hard I thought it would pop right out of my chest.

"There aren't many foster homes. If they're full, well then—"

"Don't worry. We won't let that happen," interrupted Sophia.

Poor Anton looked up at me with huge eyes and a dropped jaw.

"Won't let that happen," I muttered to him.

Just then a man entered the room.

"No, we could not! Hello boys, I'm Sophia's husband, Daniel. *Laskavo prosymo* (Welcome), we hope to make you as comfortable as possible while you're staying with us." He held out his hand to me. I reached out, and we shook hands.

"You must be Alex." He was a big man, very tall and stocky. His head was bald, but he sported a beard. He then reached out to Anton.

As they shook hands, he saw that Anton was

looking at his bald head with curiosity. Baldness wasn't a common sight in our neighborhood. Daniel smiled at Anton and rubbed his bald head.

"No hair, like a new baby, huh? It seems it fell off my head and landed on my face!" He laughed. "Rub it, and you will have good luck!"

Daniel bent over so Anton could reach the top of his head. He looked up at me, not sure what to do. I smiled and nodded, then rubbed Daniel's head. Anton rubbed it, too. We all laughed.

"Come with me. I'll show you where you'll be staying," said Sophia. We all followed her into one of the two bedrooms at the very back of the house (Sophia told us their room was at the front of the house and off limits to all children). It was a small room, painted a soft yellow. One wall featured a bright, colorful mural of a field of sunflowers.

"Wow! That's beautiful. I never saw anything like that in a house."

"Thank you, Anton," said Sophia.

"Sophia painted that herself," boasted Daniel. "There's one of a barnyard in the other room, complete with goats and chickens. She's a very talented artist, among other things. She's also a great cook," he said proudly. Sophia smiled lovingly at her husband.

Along the opposite wall were two cribs and a small bed. On another wall was a dresser that also served as a changing table.

"Do we have to sleep in those? I don't think we can fit," Anton asked sincerely.

Sophia smiled comfortingly. "We have two folding beds to set up for you. Daniel will be moving the cribs into the other room. Little Michael will stay in here. That's his big-boy bed. He just started sleeping in it. It will be a bit crowded, but we can make it work. Just put your things there for now."

Anton and I put our stuff on the floor next to the door where Sophia had gestured.

"Well, I'll be going then. I think you're in good hands," said Anna.

"What about Irina?" I asked nervously.

"I'm going to the hospital now."

"I want to come."

"No," Anna said gently, "you stay here and take care of your brother. He needs you right now, Alex."

"Why don't you boys go and watch some television with the other children, while I walk Anna to the door," said Sophia.

Anton and I went meekly into the living room and sat on the couch. It was a warm, homey room with flowered wallpaper, small pink and white flowers in clusters, growing on green leafy vines. There was a tan couch to the side, and there were two matching chairs in the center. A table with a white lamp sat between the chairs. The television was in the middle of the far wall, and there was a playpen for the kids in front of it.

On the television screen, three puppet animals were singing a counting song. Tanya was now sitting in a bouncy chair that allowed her the freedom to roam around. Three other little kids were watching the TV. One was a girl, a little older than Tanya. She was in the playpen. A boy I guessed was Michael and girl were sharing one of the chairs and singing the number song along with the puppets on the screen.

Tanya bounced her way closer, and Anton slipped off the couch onto the floor to play with her. The walker had a tray in the front and some toys attached. Anton began hitting them so they would spring back and rattle. Tanya was giggling excitedly, clapping her hands and bouncing up and down. I think Anton was having as much fun as she was. It was the first time I heard him laugh, genuinely laugh for quite a while.

Sophia came back in from outside where she and Anna had been saying their good-byes. She saw Anton and Tanya playing and smiled.

"I see you're getting acquainted with Tanya. It looks like you're becoming fast friends." She winked at Anton, who turned a bright shade of red and grinned.

"This is Sasha, in the playpen. She's two years old, and she likes to lay down in there while she watches the television. We think it makes her feel safe. And these two big kids are Michael and Yana. They're three-year-old twins."

"Yana? That was our mother's name."

"It's a beautiful name," replied Sophia.

As if to change the subject, she asked if we were hungry. I hadn't thought about food, but now that she mentioned it, yes, I was.

"I could eat," I answered.

"Me, too!" said Anton.

"Me, too, me, too!" mimicked the twins.

"Good," laughed Sophia. "Dinner will be in about half an hour. Do you like *srazy?"*

Did we! They were delicious meat pies with rice, not something Irina had mastered in her pursuit of the culinary arts. Dinner was going to be a real treat!

"Yes, we love *srazy!"*

"Excellent. If you eat a good dinner, we have *kutia* (a sweet grain pudding) for dessert. Anton, if you could continue to entertain Tanya, Alex will help set the table."

***

The twins were sitting on booster seats on one side of the table, and Anton and I sat opposite them. Tanya and Sasha were in high chairs at either end, Tanya next to Daniel, and Sasha next to Sophia. The table was full of pies, lemonade, and a plate of assorted fresh fruits, all ready for us to enjoy. *This is what it's like to be a family. Everyone sitting around a dinner table, and sharing a meal of good food.* I thought.

Another memory rushed through the back my mind. It was of dinners past: Papa sitting at one end of the table, Mama at the other, bowing her head while Papa said a prayer. Eating, laughing, Anton throwing food from his high chair, Mama scolding him, but not really mad.

"Let's bow our heads," said Daniel, bringing me back to the present.

"O Christ God, bless this food and drink for Your servants, for You are holy, always, now and forever and ever. Amen."

I dove into the *srazy* like I hadn't eaten in days!

"Well, I finished moving the cribs, and I put all of Yana's clothes into the girl's dresser, so there will be room for your things, boys. After supper you can unpack and get yourselves settled in," said Daniel.

"I'm so glad you were here to help, D. Thank you," smiled Sophia.

Daniel gave his wife a nod. "My ultimate and supreme pleasure!" He gave an exaggerated wave of his arm and pretended to bow.

"How's the food, boys?" asked Daniel.

"Umm, really good," said Anton. My mouth was so full that I couldn't answer, so I just grunted with a nod.

"Have another." Sophia took another pie and

placed it on my plate. I managed a thank you in between bites.

When we had finished our meal, Sophia said she was going to clean up and get the little ones bathed and ready for bed.

"I'll give you a hand," said Daniel. "Then we'll have dessert in front of the television. You, boys, take your dishes to the sink, and go to your room and get settled in, OK?"

After we had cleared our dishes, we went to our temporary room and started unpacking.

"That was a good dinner, wasn't it, Alex?"

"You bet. I can't wait to taste Sophia's *kutia!*"

"Have I ever had *kutia*? I can't remember it." Anton pulled out his clothes and started putting them in the bottom drawer.

"Is it OK if I take the two bottom ones?"

"Sure, I'll take the two on the top. It doesn't matter. We probably won't be here that long anyway.

"Mrs. Babich made us *kutia* on Christmas a couple of years ago, remember?"

"Oh, yes," Anton said, "it was so thick and

sweet."

After we finished putting our few things away, we sat down on our beds and waited. I got out my comics and started reading. Anton was playing with his toy soldiers on the floor when we heard Daniel call.

"Who's ready for dessert?"

We jumped up. "Coming!"

Dessert was just as delicious as dinner had been. Daniel was right about Sophia's cooking.

We watched a video, and then Sophia turned on a news show. Anton and I were both very tired, so Sophia walked us to the bedroom and checked to see if we had enough blankets and pillows.

She said goodnight and left.

We changed into our night-clothes and got into bed. Now that it was dark and quiet, the events of the day finally hit us.

"Alex?"

"Yeah, you OK?"

"I'm OK. Do you think Irina will be here soon?"

"You heard what Anna said. She has to stay in

the hospital for a few days at least. Maybe by the end of the week. Who knows? We might be home by then, and everything will be the way it was," I told him.

"Do you think Papa is still in jail?"

"I don't know, Anton, maybe. We'll probably know more tomorrow."

"Did you see what Papa did to her? How could he do that?"

I didn't have an answer for him. I just told him that Papa was drunk.

"Alex, can I come over with you?"

"Sure, come on." We both lay in bed and cried, silently, in the dark.

I fell asleep with the news on the television in the background; "Protests in the capital city of Kharvisk continued today…"

CHAPTER 4

The Suspension

I woke up to the sound of Anton screaming in his sleep. This was the third night in a row.

Michael couldn't sleep with the disturbances, so Sophia moved him next door with his sister. He didn't mind. He was happy to be back with his sister.

I quickly went to Anton's bed and rubbed his back until he woke up. Mama would always tell us to repeat our nightmares out loud, then finish the story with a happy ending. She said that way when we went back to sleep we wouldn't go back into the same dream again. So that's what I did with Anton.

"It's OK. You had a bad dream. Was it the same one about Papa beating Irina?"

That had been last night's dream. In the one before he had dreamed that he went into the forest with Irina and me for a picnic. He ran ahead, and when he turned around, we were gone. He was lost and alone in the woods.

"No, it was different," he said.

"Tell me, come on."

He sat up.

"Irina was walking with me by a lake, holding my hand. Then she stopped, turned to me and said *I have to go now, Anton*. I told her she couldn't go because I didn't know how to get home without her. *You'll be fine; you have to let me go.* Then she started to fade away. I tried to hold on to her, but she just kept fading until she was gone." He was sobbing.

"OK, keep going and give it a happy ending."

"I can't," he said weakly.

"Come on. It'll make you feel better."

"No, Alex, I can't. Just let me be."

***

For nearly a week, we waited to hear about Irina and about when we would be going home. Sophia said she was concerned about Anton's nightmares and was going to call Anna.

"She will know what's going on," she told me.

That afternoon, Anna returned Sophia's call. When Sophia hung up, she called Anton and me into the living room.

"Sit down, boys. I have some news for you," she

said.

I tried to read her expression, but couldn't tell if it would be good news or bad news. We sat down on the couch.

"I just spoke with Anna." *Come on we know that much. Get to the point,* I thought.

"Irina is doing much better, and she should be out of the hospital in a day or so."

"That's good news, right?" asked Anton. "What about Papa?"

"Well, he was released the next morning, after he sobered up."

"Why hasn't he come for us?" I asked.

"He can't just come for you, Alex. You're in the custody of the state. The Government Division of Child Protection placed you in foster care until the courts decide if it's safe for you to go home.

"You'll be going to a hearing," she continued, "that's a meeting of sorts at the courthouse. A judge will check reports, ask some questions, and decide when it will best for you children to go home."

Go home, I thought. *What would happen when we got there? Would Papa be drunk and furious about all this?* I looked over at my little brother. I never thought about how young he was. So young to have been through so much.

"You OK?" I knew Anton was having the same thoughts about going back to our house. But we had been through Papa's anger before. At least we would all be home and together.

Life here with Sophia and Daniel was fantastic! But we knew it wasn't our life. For me, it was just a reminder of what we lost a long time ago; for Anton, it was a taste of what would never be for us.

"It's getting late. I had better start supper," said Sophia. "Daniel should be home from work in about an hour. You be good and play nice while I cook, OK?" she told the younger ones.

"I'll stay here with them," said Anton.

"Wonderful, Anton, thank you. You're always so helpful. I think that I'll make a special dessert tonight, just for you!"

"Like what?" he asked with a big smile.

"Well, let me see…Like angel wings covered with sugar."

"Wow!" said Anton. "Angel wings are my very favorite dessert!"

"So a little bird told me." She winked at me and went into the kitchen to prepare supper.

When Daniel got home, the table was set, and dinner was ready to serve.

Once we were all settled, Daniel said a prayer, and then Sophia filled a plate with homemade sausage and potato pancakes and passed it to Daniel.

She did the same for the rest of us, except for Tanya, who didn't have enough teeth to chew sausage. She got potato pancakes and applesauce. There were sliced fresh tomatoes on the table from Sophia's garden. The last of the season.

"Sophia tells me that your sister is doing well, Alex. That is indeed good news," Daniel said between chews.

"D, manners please in front of the children."

"Of course, my dear," he answered, and then he let out the loudest burp I had ever heard!

"Daniel!" Sophia seemed to be angry, but when we all started laughing, she couldn't help but smile and shake her head.

"When I spoke to Anna today, she said it might take anywhere from a few weeks to a couple of

43

months, to get a date for the hearing. She suggested we put the boys back in school," Sophia said.

"Good idea," Daniel agreed. "I'll go into the factory a little late tomorrow, so I can take them in, and speak to the director.

"How does that sound to you, Alex?"

"Sounds good."

"Anton?"

"Great, I miss my friends."

***

The next morning, we had oatmeal and juice for breakfast, which we ate in record time. We grabbed our backpacks and headed to the car. We were excited to get back to school and to see our friends.

When we got there, Anton and I sat in the outer office, while Daniel went inside to speak with Mrs. Palko, the school director. After a few minutes, they both came out.

"All set," said Daniel. "Do you remember your way back to the house?"

"Yes, we'll be all right," I told him.

"Very well then," said Mrs. Palko. "Report to

your classrooms. I've spoken to your teachers, and they're expecting you back."

We thanked her and left the office. Before we went our separate ways, I told Anton to meet me on the front steps right after school. I watched him go down the hall for a minute, then turned and went to my class.

I knocked first and then walked into the classroom. My teacher, Mrs. Olesky, looked over, welcomed me back, and told me to take a seat.

I spotted an empty desk toward the back of the room. While I was I walking through the rows of students, I heard whispering and giggling.

As I took my seat, Sergey Malinsky, the class troublemaker, looked at me with a sinister grin on his face. He leaned over to some of his friends and said something I didn't hear. More looks, more giggling.

"Something you'd like to share with the class, Mr. Malinski?" Mrs. Olesky asked.

"No." He looked down at his desk.

"Then I suggest you be quiet and pay attention."

***

The lunch bell went off at noon. As soon as Mrs. Olesky dismissed the class, we all headed to the lunch room.

As I was walking with my friend, Maks, Sergey and two of his "followers" came up behind us.

"Hey, Krisko, where ya been all week?" I tried to ignore him.

"Krisko, I asked you a question. What's the matter, don't you want to answer?"

"Maybe he doesn't want to talk about it," said one of the others. "Is that it, Krisko? Something you don't want to talk about?"

"I heard your father put your sister in the hospital. Is that why you can't go home, because your drunk old man beat up your sister, or you scared he'll beat you up, too?" Sergey laughed.

"That's enough, Sergey. Let it go, will ya?" I stopped walking and turned to face him.

"Aw, don't be so touchy, Krisko. Don't they teach you any manners in the state home?"

He turned to his group and started to laugh. When he turned back, my fist was waiting! I got him right in the mouth, and he was bleeding. The next thing I knew, more punches were thrown, and we were rolling on the floor. Kids were yelling and cheering. Just then, I felt someone pulling me up by the back of my shirt, and in a second, I saw the football coach dragging Sergey away. The fight was over. Coach and one of his assistants had heard the ruckus and seemed to appear out of nowhere, as did Mrs. Palko.

"Report to my office, both of you!" she said, sternly.

Mrs. Palko called Daniel to the school. He didn't look happy. I wondered what he was going to do with me. I had never gotten the chance to explain what had caused the fight.

"And I have no choice but to suspend both students for three days." Mrs. Palko's voice echoed in my head. *Suspend for three days, suspend for three days. When Papa hears about this, he's gonna kill me!*

Daniel asked if Anton could be dismissed early. With me suspended, there was no one to walk him back to the house, and Daniel had to return to work at the factory. He couldn't come back in time to pick him up.

The ride home seemed to take hours, even though it was only minutes. No one spoke. Even Anton held back from asking a series of questions like he usually did.

When we got back to the house, Anton went right to the bedroom, I tried to follow, but Daniel stopped me.

"Alex, come and sit at the table. We need to talk."

Sophia was already in the kitchen, waiting. The younger kids were playing in the living room. I sat down and waited for what was to come. I began rocking and chewing my thumbnail. *What if they threw me out? Anton would be alone. Where would I be sent? To jail?*

"What happened?" asked Sophia. I looked over at Daniel and back to Sophia.

"Well?" said Daniel.

"You want to hear my side?"

"You're the only one sitting here," said Sophia. "How many times have you been in trouble for fighting?"

"Never, I swear!"

"Then what happened?" repeated Sophia.

I told them exactly what had happened. About the whispering and giggling in the class, and the confrontation in the hall. They both listened without interrupting me. I wasn't accustomed to being treated with so much respect by an adult.

"Fighting accomplishes nothing," said Sophia.

"Except getting you suspended from school," added Daniel.

"I know. I shouldn't have taken a punch, but he just got to me, talking about my family that way. It won't happen again. I'm sorry."

Daniel nodded.

"OK, this is what's going to happen. For the three days you're suspended, you'll walk Anton to school every morning. You'll come straight back and scrape the house for painting. When you finish with the scraping, you'll tape off the windows and start painting the trim.

"You'll walk to school every afternoon to pick up your brother and walk him back. Got it?"

"Yes, sir. Is that it?"

"That's it. No more fighting, right?"

I couldn't believe my luck. I accepted my punishment with gratitude. It could have been so much worse.

"I promise."

I started to leave, then I stopped and turned.

"Daniel, Sophia? Thank you for–well–for everything, just everything.

CHAPTER 5

The Reunion

The first day of my suspension was uneventful. I got up early and walked Anton to school. It was farther away than from our house. It took us an extra fifteen minutes each way to get there. Anton, as always, was full of questions.

"Alex, when is Irina coming to the foster home to be with us?"

"Sophia said pretty soon. She's doing much better."

"What do you think Papa will do to us when we do get home? He's gonna be awful mad."

"I know he'll be mad, Anton, but I don't think he'll beat us like he did Irina. The police would lock him up again, and he probably wouldn't get out the next morning like he did this time."

Finally, we arrived at school.

"Here we are. Meet me after school right over there by that tree, and if I'm a little late just wait for me. Don't try to walk back by yourself."

Anton looked at the doors to the school but didn't make a move to go in.

"What's wrong?" I asked.

"I'm kind of scared, Alex. What if Sergey's friends come after me? I'm not big enough to fight them."

"I promised Sophia and Daniel that there would be no more fighting. That goes for you, too. I'm afraid that if we give them any more trouble, they're not gonna let us stay."

"So, what can I do?"

"Head to the first adult you see. If you don't see one, run as fast as you can to the office. They won't bother you there. By the time Sergey comes back, I'll be back, too."

"Right. OK, I'm off." He paused and said, "Umm, you won't tell...about me being scared, I mean."

"Relax, Anton; it's nothing to be ashamed of; we're all afraid of something, even grownups."

"Even Papa?"

"Yes, even Papa. And no, I won't tell. Now go before you're late for class."

I watched him walk into school, wishing I hadn't gotten in trouble. *You should be there to protect him,* I thought.

I walked away feeling guilty.

When I got back, I started in right away, gathering the tools Daniel had left me, and scraping off the old chipped paint.

The morning flew by. Sophia called me in for lunch.

"How's it going out there?" she asked while she placed a plate of sausage and a *bublik*, (a bread roll similar to a bagel) on the table. I finished washing up at the sink and sat down.

"It's going pretty good. What color are you gonna paint the house?"

"The same, white with green trim. We just want to freshen it up. I've meant to ask, how do you think Anton is doing?" Sophia looked genuinely concerned. She was such a kind lady.

"He's afraid of everything...that Irina won't be with us, that Papa will beat us when we get home, that Sergey and his friends will hurt him at school," I told her.

"Well, I think I can help with at least one of those things. Anna phoned this morning. Irina is going to be discharged from the hospital after lunch. You and Anton can see her today. They should get here shortly after you both get back from school."

"Really?" I jumped up and hugged her. When I realized what I had done, I backed away and sat back down. Sensing my embarrassment, she said nothing. She just smiled as she got up from the chair. She touched my shoulder, walked over to the refrigerator, and poured me a glass of lemonade.

"As far as your father is concerned," she continued, "now that the courts know what's been going on, I'm sure they'll be checking up on you. Unless he wants to go to jail for a long time, he'll keep his fists in his pockets."

"That's what I told Anton, but I'm not sure he believed me," I said.

"Maybe it'll help if I tell him, too."

"Thank you, Sophia." *Thank you, again.*

***

After lunch, I worked on the house for a while longer and then left to pick up Anton. He was right where he was supposed to be, next to the tree. When he saw me, he came running.

"Hi!" he shouted. When he got to me, he was out of breath and smiling.

"Well, don't you look happy. How'd it go today?"

"No trouble. When Mrs. Palko saw Sergey's friends walking toward me in the hall this morning, she called them over. She told them that she would be watching for any sign of trouble, with any of the

Kriskos, and they should be on their best behavior both in and out of school."

"Good news, huh? Feel better?" I asked.

"Better," he smiled.

We got back just in time to see Anna's car pull up. I hadn't told Anton that Irina was finally coming to be with us. I wanted him to be surprised, and if anything went wrong like she couldn't come today, after all, I didn't want him to be disappointed.

The car door opened and out stepped Irina. Anton screamed her name and took off running. I was not far behind.

Irina looked much better than she had the last time we saw her, that's for sure. She had bruises, but no blood. Her eye was black with stitches above it. She walked stiffly. Sophia had told us that her ribs were wrapped, and it was apparent they were hurting her.

When Anton reached her, his excitement overcame him. He threw his arms around her and hugged her tight!

"Ouch! Easy little brother. My ribs."

Anton jumped back letting her go. He realized that he had hurt her and felt terrible. I thought he was going to cry.

"I'm so sorry, Irina. I'm so, so sorry."

"I'm all right, Anton. Get back here."

He returned to hug her, more gently this time, and she returned his affection.

Then she opened an arm and motioned for me to join them. The three of us just stood there hugging until Anna broke the spell by saying, "Shall we go inside? It's a little cold out here."

Sophia was at the front door waiting.

"Hello, Irina. I'm Sophia. Please, come on in."

We all removed our shoes, and when we got inside, I saw that there were drinks and cookies set up on the coffee table in front of the couch.

"Sit down, everyone, please."

Sophia served, and Anton started with the questions.

"Are you OK?" he asked Irina. "What was it like in the hospital?"

"I'm much better. Everyone was very nice to me at the hospital. I'm sorry you had to go through all this because of me. But I hear the people here are very nice, too."

She smiled at Sophia. "Thank you for being so kind to my brothers. I can see they've had good care."

"It's been my pleasure," smiled Sophia. She passed the cookies.

"Yes, Sophia and Daniel are very nice," I said. "Now that you're here, you can help take care of us, and we can help take care of you. I imagine we'll be going home soon, but you'll still have time to get acquainted with the little ones. They're adorable."

Irina looked over at Anna then down at the floor.

"What?" asked Anton.

"I'm afraid Irina won't be staying here. Sophia and Daniel are over their limit as it is. I've found another place for her."

"Not prison!" I jumped to my feet.

"No, of course not! I've placed her with another foster family. They've agreed to fit her in their home because it's short-term. I just wanted you to see one another before I drop her off. She'll be in another school so you won't see her for a while."

Anton began to cry. "No, that's not fair. We've been waiting for her all this time so we can be together."

"I'm sorry, kids. It has to be this way, for now. But, I do have some good news.

"We've been assigned a court date. The hearing will be in two weeks."

"How did you manage to get it so soon?" asked Sophia.

"With all the protests in the capital, the courts here have been ordered to clear their calendars of as many cases involving children as possible. Luckily, we were already on the court list for scheduling, or who knows how long we'd be waiting. It could be months, maybe even years, depending on the outcome there."

Irina smiled at us and said, "We can do two weeks, right, boys? Easy peasy!"

"Sure we can. Right, Anton?"

He nodded his head, but not too convincingly.

"Maybe I'll be able to call you from the foster home," said Irina.

"I'm sure you will," responded Anna.

"What riots are you talking about, Anna? What happened?"

"It's just politics, Alex. The people are protesting conditions. It's nothing for you to be concerned about, you have enough to deal with right now."

"We had better go, Irina. It's getting late, and they're expecting us."

We said our good-byes. It was one of the saddest things I've ever done. Anton was so hurt, it broke my heart. I could tell Irina was feeling the pain, too, in spite of the brave face she tried to put on for us.

After they had left, we went back to the bedroom. Anton pulled out his toy soldiers and sat down on the floor to set them up. I picked up an issue of Spiderman and just stared at the pictures.

We didn't talk. There wasn't much to say.

CHAPTER 6

The Hearing

The following week, I finished scraping the house, so I started taping off the windows. When that was done, I'd be ready to paint the trim. I intended to finish the house, even after my punishment was over. I enjoyed helping Sophia and Daniel. They had done so much for us.

On Wednesday, I was allowed back in school. Before I could go to class, I had to report to Mrs. Palko's office. When I got there, Sergey was sitting in the outer room. I was just about to take a seat next to him when Mrs. Palko opened her office door and called us in.

"I just want to be clear. I will not tolerate any more altercations between you two, and that includes your little entourage, Mr. Malinsky. Your next fight will result in your expulsion. Do you both understand what I'm telling you?"

We told her we did. She sent us to class.

As we walked into the classroom, Sergey stopped in the front and raised his arms like a returning hero. His friends welcomed him back with a loud chant: *Ser-gey, Ser-gey*!" Mrs. Olesky told us to take our seats and ordered the class to be quiet.

A week went by without incident. After school on the following Wednesday, we walked back to the house. Sophia gave us a snack, and we went to the bedroom to do our homework.

Just before supper, Sophia called out, "Alex, Anton, come quickly! There's a call for you."

We looked at each other, jumped up, and raced to get the phone, hearts pounding with excitement.

"Is it Irina?" Anton shouted as he entered the room at full gallop.

"Slow down, pal, before you run down my wife!" Daniel joked.

"Yes, it's Irina," Sophia said as she handed Anton the phone.

They spoke for a few minutes, and then he handed the phone to me.

"Don't hang up when you're done. I want to say good-bye again." He was so happy and excited to hear from Irina. So was I.

"Hello, Irina?"

"Alex, hello. How are you doing?"

"Great. How about you?"

"I miss you and Anton terribly, but other than that, it's not too bad here."

"Are they nice?" I asked.

"Well, they did let me call you, which was nice."

"Do they hit you?"

"Not me, but some. Are you ready for the hearing tomorrow morning? Anna is picking me up at eight o'clock, and then I guess we'll come to get you two and go to the courthouse."

"I can't wait to see you, Irina. What do you think will happen when we get home? Sophia says Papa won't dare beat us. He'd be afraid of going back to jail."

"I think she's probably right. But we should be on our best behavior. When Papa's drinking, he doesn't think straight."

"Maybe he feels bad for what he did. Maybe he'll stop drinking now, and we can be a happy family again, just like when Mama was alive."

"That would be wonderful. I guess we'll find out when we get home."

"I'll see you in the morning. Good night, Irina. I love you. Here's Anton again. He wants to say good night."

"Good night, Alex. I love you, too."

**

The next morning Anton and I got up earlier than usual. We dressed as nicely as we possibly could with the few clothes we had.

Sophia made us a special breakfast of pancakes, sausage, and fruit. By eight o'clock, we were ready and anxious to go.

Anna and Irina were right on time. As we headed off to the courthouse, Sophia and the twins stood in the doorway waving good-bye.

We pulled up to a three-story stone building. The front of the building was decorated with ornaments and statues featuring soldiers of the revolution. There were four marble columns in the center. Above the columns was the modern coat of arms of Ekrunia. Three large wooden doors led into the building. There were no special courts for children's issues. The judges here presided over all kinds of cases, from murderers to runaways.

Anna parked the car on the street next to the courthouse. We all got out and walked across the square and up to the courthouse steps. Just inside the door were six police officers checking everyone entering for weapons. Anna said the police were looking for rebels.

The interior of the building was decorated with intricate wood panels, multicolored marble and bronze artwork. We continued up the marble stairs to the courtroom of Judge Franko.

Because it was a Division of Child Protection hearing, the room wasn't open to the public. Only people involved in the case were allowed.

Inside the courtroom were ten rows of seats with aisles on either side of the room. Sitting in the front row on the right were Paul and his mom. Irina smiled when she saw them and mouthed to Paul, "I miss you." He blew her a kiss.

In the front were two large tables with chairs. Beyond them was an ornately carved, elevated desk. It was Judge Franko's bench.

As Anna walked us down the aisle on the right to a table, I noticed that someone was sitting at the table to my left. I sat down and looked over. It was Papa. He was looking straight ahead. He looked angry as usual. Just then, Anton and Irina also noticed him.

"Papa?" Irina called to him.

He did not attempt to acknowledge her. Just then Judge Franko entered. We stood, as Anna had instructed until the judge ordered us to sit down.

"Welcome back to my court, Miss Petrovich. Good to see you, again."

"Thank you, Your Honor."

Judge Franko continued. "This hearing is to determine the placement of the three minor children, Anton Krisko, age nine, Alex Krisko, age fourteen, and Irina Krisko, age fifteen. Are all the parties present?"

"Yes, Your Honor," said Anna. "As we stated in our application, the three minor children were taken into custody after an incident where the father, Mr. Igor Krisko, a single parent, was reported to the police for abuse of his daughter, Irina."

"The report states that Mr. Krisko was drunk at the time of the incident."

Judge Franko glared at Papa. He didn't seem to have much use for fathers who got drunk and beat their children.

"Yes, Your Honor, that is correct. We're here to determine when the children will be placed back in the family home. I have reports from the police, the hospital, and several neighbors. However, the court-appointed doctor has not…"

"If I could just interrupt you right there, Miss Petrovich. As of this morning, there's been a new development. Please be seated for a moment. We need to get it on the record."

"What's happening?" Irina whispered to Anna.

"I'm not sure," she whispered back.

"Mr. Igor Krisko, would you please stand before the court?"

Papa got to his feet. He still refused to look at us. We could tell he had been drinking, but to a stranger, someone who didn't know him, he seemed quite sober.

"I have here a Voluntary Termination of Parental Rights consent form, signed by Judge Bokavich just this morning.

"Is this your signature, Mr. Krisko?" The judge handed the paper to the clerk to show Papa.

"Yes, it is," said Papa.

"And are you voluntarily giving up your rights as a father to the three minor children listed in the petition?"

"Yes, I am."

At this point, we began to understand what was happening. Papa was washing his hands of us!

"No, Papa, what are you doing!" Irina screamed as Anna tried to quiet her.

"You can't just throw us away like garbage!" I yelled, "Mama would never have let this happen!"

"You shut up! I've had enough of you useless little…"

"You bastard! I'll kill you!" I felt rage coursing through my body, uncontrollable blind fury I jumped over the table. The court guard ran forward and restrained me. I struggled to get loose. Irina screamed. Paul rushed to her side and held her.

The judge was pounding his gavel on the desk, yelling for order.

"That will be enough! Miss Petrovich, control those children! Mr. Krisko. You are dismissed. You had better leave now before I have you taken into custody for disrespecting this court." Judge Franco stated flatly.

As Papa left the courtroom, he continued to look

straight ahead. Irina was hysterical. She kept yelling, "Papa, you can't do this! No, wait, Papa!" Anna was trying to calm her down.

Judge Franko slammed the gavel and yelled, "If you, children, don't calm down this minute, I will have you removed, and placed in juvenile detention!" Irina stopped screaming at Papa. She was crying uncontrollably.

"Miss Petrovich, we're going to take a fifteen-minute recess while everyone comes to terms with the events of the last few minutes. Please educate these children on courtroom etiquette. I will not tolerate further outbursts. Young man," he glared at Paul, "that goes for you as well. Get back to your seat in the gallery or face a fine." The judge stood and left.

Irina calmed down a bit. She kept asking Anna if Papa could stop being a parent just because he wanted to.

"How can he do that? How?"

I looked over at Anton. He sat there, staring at us, his eyes wide and full of fear. He was trembling. I went over and put my arm around his shoulders.

Fifteen minutes passed quickly, and suddenly, the judge was back at his bench.

He looked directly at us. "This must be very difficult for you to understand," he said, his voice full of compassion. "Your father has elected to give up all of his parental rights and turn your care over to the state. I have no alternative but to declare you social orphans."

I felt as though the life had just been sucked out of me.

"As such, I order the Government Division of Child Protection to remove the Krisko children, Irina, Alex, and Anton, from foster care and place them into a boarding school appropriate for the care of said children, as determined by the Custody and Care Authority of Luhansk Oblast. This order is to take effect three days from today.

"This matter is resolved. All parties are dismissed."

Just like that, orphans. The life we had always known, over.

What would become of us?

CHAPTER 7

Another Loss

On the ride home, we tried to digest what had taken place that morning. It was all surreal. We were orphans, not by the death of a father, but by the hatred of a father who, with the swipe of a pen, denied us our parentage.

When we got back to the house, Anna asked to speak to Sophia alone. The kids were taking their naps, so Anton and I took Irina to the back porch. We sat on the steps facing the garden in the backyard.

"What happens now?" Anton was the first to speak. Irina put her arm around him and pulled him close.

"We'll just take care of each other," said Irina.

"When Anna finishes talking to Sophia, we'll find out more about where they send orphans," I countered.

I still couldn't fathom the truth. Could the term "orphan" actually refer to us, the Krisko kids? What if the stories we had heard about orphans were true?

Before the revolution, most orphanages and boarding schools were in the country, hidden away. Now there was a boarding school right on the outskirts of Pervaiske, where orphans from all over the territory went to live. It was rumored children there were abused by staff members, and even tied up and beaten by their peers for things like getting good grades because it put pressure on others to work harder. Sometimes orphans disappeared. It was also rumored there was never enough food.

Irina knew the stories as well as I did. Anton asked once about something he had heard about punishments up there. I didn't know exactly how much he had heard. What I did know was that I was the oldest boy. It was my job now to protect my sister and brother. The problem was, I was scared to death.

Sophia came to the back door and called us in. She had made sandwiches and lemonade. We hadn't had any lunch, not that we were all that hungry.

Anna was joining us, so we all sat down at the table.

"Well, I heard you had quite a morning. I just wanted to say that you mustn't lose faith that everything will be all right." Sophia was trying to comfort us. "Let's have some lunch and talk. You must have a hundred questions for Anna."

"I'm so confused right now. I don't even know what to ask. We will stay together, right?" I asked.

Anna looked me right in the eyes.

"Alex. Let me explain a little about the system. Orphanages are divided into age groups, birth to three, three to seven, and seven to eighteen. Anton is nine, Irina is sixteen, and you're fifteen, so you will all be at the same facility. But, you will be assigned to different dormitories, You'll share common areas, and share meals together. All of you will attend school in the same building."

"We won't stay in our school?" asked Anton.

"I'm afraid not. That's not the way the system is set up."

"Of course, it's not set up that way! We're not good enough to go to our old school and socialize with normal kids anymore. We're social orphans now. That means we're not even good enough for a mean drunk to call us his children. Social orphans? More like social outcasts. Isn't that right, Anna?"

"Irina, you're overreacting…"

"Overreacting? We've just been cast aside like bags of garbage, and we're about to be locked up in an institution! Stop sugar coating it and tell the damn truth!" Irina was screaming now.

"Stop it, Irina. Shut up, just shut up!" Anton ran out. I chased him for several blocks before he finally stopped. I held him as he sobbed.

"I can't go there. I just can't, Alex. What are we gonna do?"

"I'll tell you what we're not gonna do. We're not gonna give up. We're gonna stick together and survive whatever comes, got it?" I hoped I sounded convincing.

"Got it. That's something Daniel would say." He looked up at me and tried to force a smile.

"I'll try my best, Alex. I promise."

"I know you will," I answered.

The walk back was a little cold. It was about four degrees Celsius (forty degrees Fahrenheit) out, and we were in our shirt sleeves.

When we got back to the house, Anna had already left to take Irina back to the foster home. Anton was upset that he hadn't had a chance to say good-bye.

Sophia was warming some milk for hot chocolate to help us warm up. She finished pouring the hot chocolate into cups and told us to sit down. One of the little ones began to cry in the living room. Sophia went to check.

"How's your hot chocolate?" I asked. "Are you warming up?"

"Yeah, but my stomach kind of hurts. I don't think I can finish it." He paused for a minute and then said, "Maybe Sophia and Daniel could keep us, and then we could have a home. Maybe they could even adopt us, and we'd have a mother and father that love us. I think they love us. Don't you, Alex? They're so nice to us like a mother and father would be."

"Anton, it's not gonna happen. They can't keep us."

"But, why not?" He sounded desperate.

Just then Sophia came back into the kitchen with Sasha, who had fallen in the playpen, and hit her lip on a toy. Sophia put her in the high chair and gave her a cold washcloth with ice wrapped inside to suck on. She had overheard Anton talking.

"I'm sorry. I couldn't help but hear what you two were saying. It's not that we don't care about you, we do. If we were allowed keep you, we would think about it carefully. But in our country when you apply to be foster parents, you must sign a paper that says you cannot adopt your foster children. Even if we were allowed to adopt, children with no living parents go on the list first. Plus, social orphans have to be pronounced eligible for adoption by the courts. You're not eligible to be adopted right now."

Anton looked disheartened. My heart ached for him, but I had no idea what to say. I wished Irina was there. She always knew what to say to make him feel better.

"Can I go?" he whispered.

"Of course," said Sophia.

As he left to go to the bedroom, Sophia told me to go with him and make sure he was all right.

Anton lay on the bed, staring at the mural of sunflowers on the wall. I sat down on the floor and started doing homework. I tried to make small talk, but he didn't respond.

Later, when Sophia called us to supper, he said his stomach hurt and refused to come and eat. Sophia said she would bring me a plate so I could stay with him. I wasn't very hungry, either. I pushed the food around on the plate for a while, set it on the dresser, and grabbed a pile of Spiderman comics. I took them over to Anton's bed, lay beside him, and started reading out loud. He sat up without saying a word and leaned his head on my shoulder. I read to him well past the time he had fallen asleep. Eventually, I fell asleep.

***

The next day was Saturday. Daniel usually worked on Saturdays, but this day he stayed home, I think to help us keep our minds busy.

We spent the morning painting the house. Anton had never painted a house or anything for that matter. He was a bit sloppy. Daniel and I began teasing him about painting the plants, his shoes, and even his face! He got into it and teased us back, about every drip and smudge. He said that Daniel's only work of art was the ladder, which had years of paint drips from every job Daniel had ever done, inside and out.

Sophia called us for lunch. Before we went in, Daniel said we should clean up for the day.

"But it's early. We could get a lot more done before dark," I said.

"No, that's enough for today," he told us.

So, we cleaned up and went into the house. We sat down to a lunch of *borscht*, a delicious beet soup, and fresh bread. It was cold outside, and the soup warmed us up.

"There's a football game at the school this afternoon. I thought we could go. What do you say, boys?"

"You bet!" said Anton.

"Sounds great!" I answered.

We finished lunch and helped Sophia clean up. We dressed in warm clothes. Sophia decided to stay home. Tanya had a cold, and the twins were coming down with it, also. So, it was just us guys.

It was an exciting game. Our home team won by just one point after trailing behind most of the game. We yelled so loud during the second half that we were hoarse.

We got home late for supper. Sophia had already fed the other kids and put them to bed early. We were still excited about the game and recapped every play for her while we ate.

After dinner, we sat down to watch a video. The next thing I remember was Daniel waking us up to go to bed. Both Anton and I had fallen asleep before the movie had even started!

We went into the bedroom, changed, and got into bed. As I said goodnight to Anton and rolled over to go to sleep, the thought suddenly crossed my mind; *I haven't thought of the boarding school all day.*

***

It was a lazy, quiet Sunday. We all slept in late, even the little kids. After breakfast, which was closer to lunch, Anton and I played some ball with Michael and Yana. They weren't feeling that well, so after a while, they went in to take a nap. Anton and I were kicking the football around in the street in front of the house, trying not to think about what was going to happen tomorrow. Sophia came to the door and called me in.

"What's up?" I asked her.

"Telephone."

"Irina?"

THE ARMY OF ORPHANS: The Beginning

"Yes." Sophia looked concerned.

I turned to call Anton, and she stopped me.

"She said she only wants to talk to you, Alex."

That was strange. Irina always spoke with Anton first. When I went in, I could hear Sophia talking to Anton outside. Then she started kicking the ball around with him.

"Hello?"

"Alex, it's me," said Irina. "I have to talk to you, and I need you to listen, just listen until I'm finished. Will you do that for me?"

"You sound so serious, has something else happened? Are you all right?"

"I'm fine. Just please, listen."

"OK, I'm listening."

"I can't do it, Alex. I can't go to the boarding school. I can't live like an orphan. I've heard the stories about the girls my age. I can't go through it!"

"I don't understand Irina. What choice do you have?"

"I have a choice Alex. Paul is taking me away."

"What!"

Just then Daniel hollered from the kitchen, "Everything all right out there?" I realized that I must have been speaking very loudly. I yelled back that everything was fine.

I cupped my hand over the mouthpiece and continued.

"What are you saying?"

"I'm saying that Paul and I have run away. We're going to get married, and we're not coming back for a time. When I'm eighteen, I'll come back for you and Anton, I swear."

I could hear a loudspeaker in the background announcing departures. They were already at the train station.

"Irina, what about Anton? You can't do this to him! He's already been through so much. I'm afraid if you disappear it'll push him over the edge! Please, don't do this!"

"I'm sorry, Alex. This is my only choice. Please, if you love me, you have to understand."

"I do love you, Irina, but I don't understand. If you care anything for Anton, you won't do this to him. He needs you, and he'll never understand how the closest thing to a mother he's ever had could abandon him. First Papa, now you. How can you just walk away from us?" I felt desperate.

"Alex, please, you're just not being fair…"

"Fair! You talk to me about being fair?"

Just then I heard Paul's voice in the background, telling Irina that they had to go, quickly.

"I have to go, Alex. We need time to get away. You can't tell anyone. Please."

And the line went dead.

CHAPTER 8

The Boarding School

The three days since the court order was issued passed quickly. It was Monday morning. Anton and I were getting ready to move to the boarding school. I still hadn't said anything to him about Irina. He was expecting her to be with Anna when she arrived. I didn't know what to do. I promised that I wouldn't tell anyone what Irina said on the phone the day before, that she was running away. I figured she and Paul had a good enough head start, so I decided to ask Sophia for help.

I told Anton that I was going to check what time Anna was supposed to be there. I went into the kitchen where Sophia was preparing breakfast.

"Sophia, can I talk to you for a minute?"

"Of course, Alex." She turned and looked at me. A soon as she saw my face, her expression changed. She looked concerned.

"Let's sit down. What's going on?" Sophia asked.

"Well, I um…" I was stammering. I was nervous.

Afraid Sophia would be mad at me for not telling her.

"Remember when Irina called yesterday? Well, she was calling from a pay phone at the train station. She ran away with Paul. This is going to kill Anton. I don't know what to do."

Sophia sat back and let out a sigh.

"You have to tell him. He'll know soon enough, and he has to know he can always trust you to be honest with him." She paused a moment, then continued. "Where were they going?"

"She didn't tell me, and I was too upset to think to ask her," I answered.

"Why didn't you say something yesterday?" asked Sophia.

"She begged me not to; she told me they needed time to get away. But now I have to think about Anton and what I'm going to say to him."

"The truth, that's all you can say," Sophia said. "Would you like me to be with you while you talk to him?"

I nodded, and Sophia went with me to the bedroom where Anton was still packing. As we came in, he looked up.

"Irina's gone away with Paul," I said, sitting down. "They ran away yesterday, and I don't know where they went."

He just stood there.

"Did you hear what I said?"

"Yup," he answered and went back to packing. I looked over at Sophia. His reaction was not what we were expecting.

"Do you want to talk about it?" asked Sophia.

"Nope."

"Anton, do you understand what's going on? Irina is gone!" I said. My palms were sweating.

"I heard you, but what can I do about it? I couldn't stop Papa from beating her or throwing us away. I can't do anything about going to the home, and I can't do anything about Irina and Paul!" He was screaming.

When he calmed down, he said, "I hope they'll be OK."

I took his hand and pulled him down next to me.

"What's going on with you? Are you OK?"

He looked up at me with tears in his eyes. My heart was breaking for both of us. I felt helpless.

Damn it, Irina! Why did you have to put him through this?

"I guess I've been thinking a lot about everything that's happened. I wanna think it's not all bad. We did get away from Papa. You know, he didn't love us. He was mean, yelling and hitting us all the time. I figure, what can be worse than that? At least we're going through it together, or that's what I thought. I never figured on Irina leaving." He thought for a minute. "Promise you won't leave me, too, OK Alex?"

"I more than a promise I swear on my life." I took him in my arms and held him.

"I think I know why Irina left, Alex. Maybe it's because she has someone who loves her as much as we do, but he wants to take care of her for a change. It must've been hard for her to take care of us all this time. Now she has a chance to be happy. As long as us guys stick together, we'll be OK, too." He pulled back and gave me a half-hearted smile.

"But I'll miss her." He wiped the tears from his eyes.

I stared at him in disbelief. When did he get so smart and grown-up?

There was a knock on the door. Sophia put her hand on my shoulder, smiled, nodded, and went to answer. It was Anna.

We finished getting our stuff together and gave the room one last look.

"Ready?" I asked Anton.

With a big smile on his face, he took a deep breath and said, "Ready!"

We walked out onto the porch where everyone was waiting for us.

"You haven't asked about Irina." Anna looked at us suspiciously.

Anton and I looked down and said nothing.

"Say your good-byes and get in the car."

Leaving the kids was hard. Tanya and Sasha didn't understand it was our last good-bye, but Michael and Yana both cried.

As we drove away from Sophia's and Daniel's house, we waved out the back window of the car. I had a lump in my throat, but I was determined not to cry in front of Anton.

We would never forget the time we had spent with Sophia and Daniel. They would always be very special to us.

***

We arrived at the boarding school just before lunch. A six-foot wall surrounded the building and grounds. There was a large set of gates, which were already open as if someone had seen us coming. On the wall next to the entrance was a sign. It said 'Luhansk Boarding School for Orphaned and Abandoned Children.'

An uncomfortable premonition suddenly overcame me. *Something awful is going to happen. This is a bad place.*

Anna pulled into the driveway and through the gate. We followed the circular drive up to the front door. The grounds looked neglected, but it was hard to tell how badly. It was the middle of November. The tall grass (or were they weeds?) was brown, and fallen leaves were scattered across the grounds. On the side of the building were the remains of last summer's vegetable garden, which appeared to continue around to the back.

The building itself was an old three-story factory from before the revolution. Anna said it had been one of the largest producers of nitrogen fertilizers in the former Ukraine. There was always the risk of explosion associated with storing nitrogen fertilizer, and there were many environmental and health risks from its use. Because of the dangers, the plant was not reopened for manufacturing by the new government. It had been cleaned up and repurposed to accommodate the orphans.

"The front half of the building is the orphanage, and the back of the building is the school," said Anna.

"On the first floor are offices, storerooms, staff accommodations, and a small kitchen. The second floor has the dorms and bathrooms, and the third floor houses the common areas and the kitchen." She got out of the car.

As we walked to the front door, Anna leaned over and whispered, "You know, you should have told someone about Paul and Irina."

"I couldn't. I promised."

Inside the door was a small vestibule with several offices. The first of those offices belonged to the director of Luhansk Boarding School, Mr. Andrey Evanko.

Anna knocked on the door. Mr. Evanko opened the door and stepped out.

He was a burly man, tall and robust! I guessed he was in his late forties. His hair was cut short with gray on the sides, and he had a scar on his right cheek. He was wearing a dark blue suit that had seen better days.

"Hello, Anna. How are you?"

"Fine, Andrey, thank you. These are the Krisko boys."

"Do you have their paperwork?" I don't know why he asked. She was holding the file in her hand.

"Right here," said Anna.

"OK, we'll take it from here," he said.

Anna walked over to us. "Mr. Evanko will take charge from here. Good luck, boys."

She smiled at us, said good-bye, and left.

"In my office."

We followed Mr. Evanko into his office, and he motioned for us to sit down.

"I don't know what you expect here, but you're not on vacation. You will be assigned a schedule, a bed, a classroom, and a job. All the rules are posted. You will read them, and you will follow them. If you do not follow each and every rule, there will be consequences, and you have my word, you won't like them. You can expect to be here until you're eighteen years old. If there are no questions, you can wait in the vestibule while I call your dorm supervisors."

He reached for the phone and dialed.

Apparently, there were no questions!

.

CHAPTER 9
Getting Adapted

The first supervisor to come for us was an older lady. She was short and a little bulky. Her hips were the same size as her waist. Her hair was gray. It was pulled straight back from her round face and fastened in a bun. She gave a kind smile as she entered the vestibule.

"This handsome fellow must be Anton."

"Yes Ma'am," he stood up to address her.

"And with such lovely manners too. My name is Mrs. Galey, and I'm in charge of your dormitory. That's your living quarters. Have you got your things?"

"Yes," Anton answered. "Is Alex coming too?"

Just then someone else entered the vestibule. Mrs. Galey glanced his way, and with a frosty tone in her voice she said, "Denis…" She immediately looked back to Anton. She didn't wait for a response.

"Not to your dorm, dear. Alex will be sleeping with the older boys. You can visit his dorm later. Now let's get you assigned a bed. We don't want to be late for lunch."

She turned to me and said pleasantly, "We'll see you in the dining room for lunch."

When they left, the guy she called Denis looked at me and said, "That old bitch should have been put to pasture years ago." He smiled. It wasn't a very genuine smile.

"Alex Krisko?" he asked.

"That's me," I answered.

"My name is Denis Janko. You'll address me as Mr. Janko."

Denis or should I say, Mr. Janko was young. Like barely in his twenties young. He looked more like one of the older kids than he did a caretaker. He was well built and athletic. He had very fair skin and blonde hair.

"You'll be in my dorm. Let's walk, and I'll go over some of the rules."

We headed down the hall to a flight of stairs and walked up to the second floor. Off the landing were three hallways that led to the dorms. There were signs on the walls next to each one. The hall to the left had a sign that said 'primary dormitories.' The hall in the center said 'secondary dormitories,' and the one to the right was for the 'upper secondary Dormitories.' All the walls of the building were a peeling, faded gray.

"The dorms are set up according to school placement. We have two areas in each dorm. One is for the boys, and one is for the girls. The primary dorms are for boys and girls from first to fourth grade. Secondary dorms are for fifth to ninth grades and the upper secondary dorms are for tenth grade and eleventh grade."

"The school is in the back, right?" I asked.

"Yup. But you have to go outside and walk around to the side of the building to get to the entrance."

We walked straight ahead to the secondary dorm. There were two doors in the hall. The one to the left was labeled girls, and the one to the right was for the boys.

"Rule number one. You're never allowed in any of the girls' dorms, and no girls are ever allowed your dorm. That's a biggie."

"Here we go," said Denis. I mean Mr. Janko. It was going to be hard getting used to addressing someone that young as mister.

"Home sweet home." He finished with a slap on my back, opened the door, and walked down the aisle of beds that lined two walls.

"This one is yours." He sat on one of the beds.

I looked around at what was going to be my home until my eighteenth birthday. It was crowded and dimly lit. It was situated in the heart of the building, so there were no windows.

I counted forty beds on opposite sides of the room, twenty on each side. On either side of the doorway were built-in shelves sectioned off into cubes. Each cube was labeled with a name, and a cardboard box was inside. At the end of the room was a large community bathroom. My bed was right next to it.

"Lovely," I said flatly.

"What's this? Do I have a smart ass in my charge? Are you a smart ass, Alex Krisko?"

"What? No! It's just that—well, a lot of people sleep in here. There's not much privacy, and there's no door on the bathroom," I answered.

He sat there and stared at me for what seemed

like an eternity. Then he smiled that same sarcastic smile he had earlier.

"Well, I hope not. I *do* know how to handle a smart ass. I learned from the best. And keep this in mind. If you're unhappy with the accommodations, it can get a lot worse."

He got up and started pacing around the room, still smiling.

"You come back to the dorm for bed at nine thirty and lights are out at ten. You'll get up at seven at which time you will wash, brush your teeth, dress, and make your bed. Then you'll report to the third floor for breakfast. Your things go in the cube marked with your name. You leave nothing lying around."

He threw me a black marking pen.

"Put your name on everything, if you want to hang on to it."

"Nine-thirty is sort of early." Before I knew what happened, Janko swung around and landed a backhand right across my face!

"Another rule that's a biggie...never question me or argue with me."

I was shocked. My cheek was burning. I just stared at him blankly.

"Put your things in the box for now. It's time for lunch. I'll show you where to get your sheets when we get back."

I found my name and put my meager belongings into the box. It seemed that my premonition of fear was well founded. My mind went to Anton. Was he getting slapped around? I was worried and anxious to see him. Janko led the way back to the landing and upstairs to the common areas.

I followed him through a large area of mismatched couches, chairs, and tables. The rugs were faded and worn like everything else here. There was an old television off to the side of the room. More chairs and couches surrounded it. I wanted to ask if it worked but thought better of it. I didn't need another backhand. Half my face was already swollen and sore.

The dining room at the far end of the third floor was like a school cafeteria. It had a dozen or so long tables that sat ten people on each side. To the left was the kitchen. A long-serving area separated it from the dining area. This room was full of kids who were sitting at tables and standing in the serving line.

"You clean up your tray when you're done," said Janko. "Right over there's a place for plates, forks... well, you'll see it. Enjoy your lunch. I'll meet you downstairs at one-thirty to finish your orientation."

After Janko left, I looked around for Anton. I saw him just coming in with Mrs. Galey. I rushed over to make sure he was alright and was relieved to see he was.

"Can I eat lunch with my brother, Mrs. Galey?" asked Anton.

"Of course, dear," she said gently, "You're free to sit anywhere you like."

She looked at me, and her expression became serious.

"What happened to your face?"

I didn't know what to say. If I told Mrs. Galey what happened and Janko found out there might be more to come. If I didn't say anything, she might get angry at me for not answering.

"Never mind," she said sadly. "I think I know. Go now and enjoy your lunch."

We got on the serving line. I passed Anton a

tray and got one for myself. The food was hot but not very appetizing. We made our way down to the cabbage soup. Next, there was bread, then greasy fried onion patties, then blood sausage. (So much for Sophia's delicious meals.) A glass of lemonade for me, a glass of juice for Anton, and we went in search of a place to sit. We found two seats next to a couple of girls.

"What *did* happen to your face?" asked Anton as soon as we were sitting.

"Nothing," I said.

"It was that Denis guy wasn't it? Why did he hit you?"

"I wish I knew. And don't let him hear you calling him Denis. He wants to be called Mr. Janko. How about Mrs. Galey? Is she ok?"

"She's nice. I think she really cares about the kids. When I had trouble making the bed she taught me an easier way. She said I'll be starting school tomorrow so it'll be ok to hang out with you this afternoon."

"Janko's making me go back to make the bed and mark my stuff. I didn't have time before lunch. When I'm done, I can meet you in your dorm, and you can show me around. Then we can go exploring. What do you say?"

"That sounds great!"

Anton took a sip of his soup and wrinkled up his nose. "Oh boy! This food is going to take some getting used to; I think it's worse than Irina's cooking!"

***

When I got back to the dorm, Denis Janko was nowhere around. I decided to mark my belongings and sort them in the box. There wasn't much to mark. I didn't want to ruin my comics. So instead of marking them I wrapped them in a shirt and hid them at the bottom of the box. I was just finishing when Mr. Janko walked in.

"Follow me," he said.

"Where are we going?" I asked.

He stopped short and turned to face me.

"What did I tell you about questioning me? Do you need reminding?" He took a step toward me.

"No. Sorry," I mumbled.

"Sorry what?" I didn't know what he was asking me. He stared at me, waiting.

"Sorry, Mr. Janko?" I took a guess. It worked.

He walked away with a grin on his face. I followed him down to the first floor to a room he called the linen closet.

"Sheets, two— pillow cover, one— blanket, one." He named off each piece as he tossed it to me. "And that takes care of your bed. Over here we have towels, one—washcloth, one. You have a toothbrush?" I nodded. "Toothpaste? No? Here."

He handed me a small tube of toothpaste and a plastic cup.

We went back to the dorm. Mr. Janko showed me where to put my cup with my toothbrush and paste inside. I hung my towel and washcloth on the bar at the foot of my bed.

He told me to make the bed and to be ready to start school in the morning. Finally, he left. I finished up and walked back to the hall that said "primary dormitories."

Anton was sitting on his bed. The room looked just like mine except for one thing. It had windows on one wall. That made it a lot brighter than my dorm. I was right about the paint. Every wall in the entire place was a peeling, faded, gray.

"This isn't bad," I said to Anton as I walked in.

"Pretty cool, huh?" He found the best in everything these days.

Mrs. Galey walked in with an armload of clothes from the laundry.

"Well hello, Alex. Are you getting settled in?"

"Yes, pretty much," I answered. I was so relieved Anton didn't have to deal with someone like Denis Janko.

"We were going to scout around if that's allowed."

"Of course. Everyone's in school right now. It would be a perfect time."

"Are we allowed to go outside?" I asked.

"Yes. Just don't try to leave the grounds. Oh, and you aren't allowed in the office area so be sure you leave by the back door near the linen closet. Do you know where that is?"

"Yes. I remember seeing it when Denis, I mean

Mr. Janko took me there for the sheets."

"Mr. Janko," she repeated. "I remember when he was just a frightened little boy like the rest of you."

"He was an orphan here?" I don't know why I was so surprised.

"Yes. But it would be wise not to mention it to him. He likes to think he's above all that now that he's in charge of something. I really shouldn't be talking so much. Go now and explore. Have some fun while you can. Back to school tomorrow."

CHAPTER 10

Getting Acquainted

Our tour didn't take long because it was cold outside.

We checked out the garden on the side. I was right. It did extend to the back. It was big enough to feed the orphanage and still preserve plenty of fruits and vegetables for winter.

We walked along the wall and found that a few hundred feet towards the back of the property it changed to rusted, steel corrugated panels. We decided to continue our exploring another time. The sun was beginning to go down, and it was time to go in and warm up.

When we went back inside, we noticed it was supper time, so we headed to the dining room. We were a couple of the first ones there. We got in line and filled our plates. The same, gross cabbage soup from lunch was still there, but more dishes had been added. There were potato pancakes, fried breaded cutlets, (more bread than cutlet), and sliced beets. None of the new stuff looked any better than the soup.

We found a seat right away. It was close to the common room and beside a window. Soon the dining room was busy with kids coming in from school. Anton and I were discussing the food when a boy about my age came over, tray in hand, and stated, "You're in my seat."

I looked up and said, "I was told to sit anywhere. There aren't any assigned seats."

"You were told wrong. You're in my seat," the boy repeated.

"Look, there are plenty of other seats at the table. Why don't you just take one of those?"

"Because *that* is my seat. Maybe you should move."

"Dmitry, why don't you just sit down and stop starting trouble?" said someone behind me.

I turned around and saw a girl who was also about my age.

"Hi. I'm Liza. Welcome to the land of bad food and bad manners."

"Hi. I'm Alex. This is my brother, Anton."

Liza came around the table and took a seat

across from me.

"The primaries don't sit with the secondaries your table is down there. Move it you little turd!" Dmitry said to Anton.

Anton started to pick up his tray. I placed my hand on his arm to stop him.

"He sits with me," I responded. I straightened up in my chair and stared him straight in the eye. I tried hard to look unafraid.

"Stop, Dmitry. I mean it!" said Liza.

He leaned in and whispered, "This isn't over." Then he took a seat on the other side of the table.

"Sorry about my brother. He has a chip on his shoulder."

"He's your brother?" I asked, "My condolences." She ignored my sarcasm and looked over at Anton.

"So Anton, how old are you?" she asked as two more kids, a boy, and a girl, joined our table.

"I'm nine," he answered proudly. As if being nine was an achievement of momentous proportions.

Liza smiled. "I was nine when I came here."

"How old was your brother?"

"None of your damn business!" bellowed Dmitry.

"Eight," Liza replied. "And how old is your brother?"

"Fourteen."

"I'm sitting right here. Anything else you want to know?" I smiled.

"I'm Misha, and I'm twelve," said the boy who just joined us.

"Why did you say that?" asked the girl who had also come over.

"What?"

"That you're twelve."

"Everyone was talking about their ages, so I figured I'd join in," Misha told the girl. He looked over at Anton and me.

"This is Natalia. She's thirteen." Natalia smacked him on the arm. He fell back in his chair and grabbed his arm. He was yowling. We all laughed. Well, all except Dmitry.

Anton took a bite of his cutlet.

"Wow! You're brave," said Natalia. "You're actually eating mystery meat? Are you sure you want to do that?"

Anton looked down at his food.

"Don't scare the boy," said Liza "No one's ever been able to prove it."

"Prove what?" Anton was getting a little anxious.

"They say it's only a coincidence," said Misha,

"But, every time someone disappears from the orphanage, we're served mystery meat for supper."

"Are you saying this cutlet was made out of a missing—?"

"Shhhhhhh!" Everyone said it at once. They all looked around as if to see if anyone had heard him.

"Whenever someone says it out loud, they're the next to disappear," whispered Natalia.

Anton looked over at me. "They're kidding. Right?"

There was dead silence around the table.

Then, "Of course we're kidding!" laughed Liza.

Everyone laughed. Anton laughed louder than anyone. Apparently, he was relieved he wouldn't need to worry about being Sunday's buffet meat!

"You didn't scare me. I knew it was just a joke!" he said. "I'm not a baby you know."

After dinner, we cleaned up our trays. I noticed everyone in the cleanup crew was a kid.

"We all work here. You'll be given work and Anton too, just like the rest of us. Just hope you don't start with bathroom duty!" warned Liza.

Once supper was over it was study time in the common room. Anton and I hadn't been to school and didn't have homework. We each took a book off the bookshelf and pretended to read. There was no talking allowed during study time.

After a while the bell rang, signaling the end of silent/study time. It was seven thirty. Liza came over and asked us if we played a card game called drunkard. Of course, we did. All kids played drunkard. It was a favorite rainy day pastime in summer camp (which was just school without the work). I looked around for Dmitry to see if he was playing, but he was nowhere around.

"Sure," I said.

"Hey guys, over here. We've got a table and a deck of cards." Misha and Natalia were on the other side of the room.

Drunkard is played with thirty-six cards, the six to the ace of each suit. The ace is high. All the cards are dealt, and each player keeps his or her cards face down. Each player plays one card in the middle, and the high card takes the trick. If there's a tie, everybody plays another card on top of the ones already played. Simple.

There's only one catch. If you play an ace and a six at the same time, the six beats the ace.

Anton was always lucky at cards and tonight was no exception! He kept getting both aces and sixes. Every time he won he would jump up and yell. "Yes, he does it again, and the crowd roars for the unbeatable Anton!"

"Check his sleeves!" yelled Misha. Liza got up, started tickling him, and pretended to check for hidden cards. Anton squealed with delight while the rest of us wailed with laughter.

The five of us played until the bell rang at nine

fifteen. It was time to clean up and report to the dorms. In the end, Anton had won two out of three games! The others couldn't believe it.

It had turned out to be a pretty good day!

When we got to the second floor, I hugged Anton and said good night. He seemed quite comfortable. He walked cheerfully down the hall to his dorm.

When we got to the girls' dorm, Misha and I said goodnight to Liza and Natalia. As we entered the door to the boys' dorm, someone grabbed me by the arm.

"I thought I told you to make your bed!" It was Janko. He was squeezing my arm so tightly; I knew it was going leave a bruise.

"But, I did," I protested.

Janko dragged me over to my bed. It was unmade. The bedding was thrown in a heap.

"Is this how you make a bed?"

"No! It was made!"

"Well, it doesn't look made to me, smart ass."

He threw me to the floor and shouted, "Make the damn bed. Now!"

I got up off the floor and went over to make the bed. I looked up and sitting on the bed across from mine was Dmitry. He was staring at me with a malicious smile. I knew in an instant what happened to the bed. What was this kid's problem? How long was he going to keep acting like a jerk?

I took a deep breath, made the bed, and went into the bathroom to brush my teeth.

"He's just an asshole," said Misha.

"Which one?" I countered.

Misha laughed. "Right," he said, "It is a tossup. You were smart not to go after Dmitry. You know it was all a setup to get you in a fight. If you bought into it, Mr. Janko would have beaten you with a belt. He likes to show the new guys that he's the boss."

We finished up and got into bed just as Janko came in to shut off the lights. He reached over to the light switch, stopped and stared at me with a sinister grin. I knew he was out to get me.

Why? Just because.

CHAPTER 11

Life at the Boarding School

Days at the orphanage were long. We got up at seven. We dressed, ate breakfast, and went to school from eight to ten. After morning classes we went to work until one. We had half an hour for lunch and were back at work until four. At four we went back to school until six, then to supper. If we hadn't finished our jobs, we would have to go back to work after supper. Otherwise, we had homework and then free time.

I had begun to think of Irina a little less every day. The more I thought about her and how she left us, the more I missed her and the angrier I became. So, I tried not to think about her at all. Anton and I didn't talk about it. But, I'm sure he was going through a little hell of his own.

I was lucky. My first job at the school was in the laundry with Liza. She knew all the shortcuts. Most nights we got to stay for study time and then we played games, mostly cards.

Anton was given a job on the cleaning crew. His duties were to vacuum and mop floors and to dust or wash the table tops in the common areas and offices. If the offices weren't empty long enough to clean during the day, his crew had to go back after supper. I tried to switch jobs with him. Unfortunately, tasks were assigned by the dorm supervisors. While Mrs. Galey was willing, Janko, ornery as always, refused. Luckily, Mrs. Galey arranged for Anton to rotate nights with some of the older kids on the crew. He hardly ever had to go back. Not all the dorm supers were as obstinate as Janko, but mostly, they were just as mean. Except for Mrs. Galey.

In the week since we arrived at the orphanage, I had managed to avoid Janko's fists. Things with Dmitry were sort of in limbo. We both knew we would have it out one day. But, not just yet. Oh, he tried to bait me nearly every day. But, I wasn't intimidated the way the other boys were. So I managed to avoid his fists as well.

The following Tuesday I was a little late getting to breakfast, but not late enough to be noticed by Janko.

While I was getting some oatmeal and juice, I noticed the kitchen ladies weren't there. Only the kids that did the cleaning were working. I saw Anton, Liza, and Natalia, and walked over to the table to sit with them.

"Good afternoon," Liza said sarcastically.

"Very funny," I replied, "where are all the supervisory units?"

"The what?" Natalia asked.

"The supervisory units, you know, the adult units that are in charge of us poor orphans!"

"Oh, those units," said Natalia.

"Don't know for sure," said Liza. "Something on the news about the prime minister cutting pays and protests in the capital."

"I heard something about protests when we first got to the foster home, and again just before we came here," I told her.

"I remember," said Anton, "Anna said it was nothing to worry about."

"Well, I guess today, the units disagree with her," said Liza.

"I hate to change the subject, but we'd better get to school. Come on Anton, I'll walk you," I told him

"I'll come, too," said Liza.

"Hold on, wait for me," called Natalia.

We walked out the side door to get to the school

entrance. Dmitry and a couple of his friends were waiting.

"Hey, big sister. What're you doing? Taking out the trash?" His friends laughed as though he had just told a joke.

"Give it a break, would you Dmitry!" I said. "You're super mouthy when your 'groupies' are right behind you. I'd like to see you one on one in a more secluded place. But you don't have the balls for that, do you?" I brushed past him hoping he wouldn't call my bluff.

"You calling me out, Alex?"

Damn! "I'm not doing anything."

He hesitated and then said, "After school. Today. You and me in the back by the bombed-out garage."

"Sure, you and me, and just a few of your closest friends," I said.

"He may be a lot of things, Alex, but my brother will fight fair. Right, brother?"

Dmitry didn't answer Liza. He looked straight at me.

"After school, we finish this once and for all.

Then I want that little piece of shit brother of yours back at the kiddie table where he belongs. And, you'll apologize to me in front of everyone for taking my seat in the dining room!"

He turned and went to the school.

Too late. I was trapped. I didn't want to fight. *If only my mouth would wait for my brain to kick in.* I was lucky. My first and only fight back at school ended before I got hurt. I couldn't think of a way to get out of this thing with Dmitry.

"He's an excellent fighter," said Liza.

"I don't care. What can he do to me? Draw blood? Break my nose?" I tried to put up a brave front.

I walked Anton to his classroom. Before he went in, he looked up and said, "I'm coming."

"I don't want you there, Anton. If Dmitry and I get caught fighting, everyone will be in as much trouble as we will."

"As long as us guys' stick together we'll be ok, remember? I'm coming."

I smiled and tousled his hair.

"Knock it off!" he said while trying to smooth it

back.

"We'll talk about it after school," I said.

***

Mr. Tom Kovalski was the eighth-grade teacher and an ok guy. As long as you paid attention in class, he didn't bother you. He did love to talk though. On this day, it was about the protests in the capital.

"Have any of you been following what's going on in our capital?"

No response.

"Does anyone here *know* what's going on in the capital?"

No response.

"Does anyone here know where the capital is?"

"Kharvisk," called someone from the back.

"Kharvisk!" shouted Mr. Kovalski. "An answer, at last! I was afraid I had a bunch of foreign guests here today. Guests who know nothing about our country!

"Yes, Nazar. Kharvisk is the capital of Ekrunia. And today our capital is full of people from our very own city of Pervaiske. They went there to join the protest."

"Why?" asked one of the students.

"To show that we support those who have been protesting, for a fair wage, on behalf of all the people," he said to a room of blank faces.

"Let me explain. This part of Ekrunia is the richest area of natural resources in our country. Coal, gas, and minerals, are all abundant in Luhansk and Donetsk. After the people's revolution, the new government took over all the mines and gas companies as well as the factories and refineries. The workers agreed to work for meager wages for a short period. How short has yet to be decided by the government. The low pay was subsidized by vouchers based on the number of people in a family. All this was necessary for our new country to recover financially and build up our treasury.

"All these years later, it's time for the people to reap some of the benefits our new freedom has to offer. But instead, the government wants to cut subsidies. And so we protest which is our right as free citizens."

He continued, "And now the president has called on parliament to pass anti-protest laws. Laws that would be similar to the ones passed by the parliament of the old Ukraine on black Thursday, back in 2014. The law would take away the right to protest and other rights, too. The people are giving them a sign of unity."

At lunch that day, the discussion was about Mr. Kovalski's lesson on politics. We were surprised we didn't we find it boring. He talked about how we were supposed to have free elections after the revolution. But free elections were manipulated to keep those with power, in power. In time, there were no more elections.

"We fought for a free country. The government can't make people work forever for next to nothing. That's slave labor!" said Natalia.

"Haven't you noticed? We work for nothing. But we can't walk around with signs to show our anger," I said.

Just then, Janko walked by and heard the tail end of our conversation.

"Are you complaining again, smart ass? We really need do something about that."

"Not complaining, sir. Just talking politics," I answered.

"And what do a bunch of bastards and orphans like you know about politics?"

"Only what Mr. Kovalski told us in class today," said Liza.

"If you ask me he's wasting his time and breath trying to teach a bunch of misfits like you. Don't you agree smart ass?"

"Yes, sir!"

Jansky stared at me for a minute. Then he walked away. He looked disappointed I hadn't given him an excuse to backhand me again.

"Aw, why don't you give it back to him? He's just aching to beat the shit out of you," said Dmitry. He was sitting at the next table.

"Don't have time," I explained. "Gotta keep my shit in place so I can keep a date. I'm going to beat the shit out of someone else after school!" *Alex, Alex, why can't you just keep your mouth shut?*

I grabbed my tray and walked away.

"You just keep dreamin' smart ass!" Dmitry yelled after me.

"Do you honestly think you can beat him?" asked Anton. We were walking down the stairs to our respective jobs.

"Don't you little brother? Where's your faith?

Look at this bicep."

I pulled up my shirt sleeve and flexed my muscle.

"Have you ever seen such a thing of beauty before?" *What the hell. Maybe if I pretend I'm not scared, after a while I'll convince myself, too,* I thought.

"Yes!" replied Anton. "On a seven-year-old girl who moved into my dorm today. Hey! If you want maybe I can talk her into taking your place."

"Now who's the smart ass?" I pretended to take a swing at him. He had no idea my stomach was trembling, and I felt sick.

When I got to the laundry, Liza was already loading one of the machines.

"If it isn't the wannabe, lightweight, secondary, champion of Luhansk Boarding School."

"Always with the jokes," I said sarcastically.

"Are you sure you want to do this?" her tone turned serious.

"What, the laundry?"

"Now who's with the jokes?" She started throwing pieces of laundry into the machine.

"Come on, Liza. You can't be mad at me. Dmitry pushed me into a corner, and you know it. If we don't settle our differences things will go on like this forever."

"What are your differences?" she asked.

"Damned if I know, Liza. Dmitry's been on my case since I got here. You were there, remember?"

"I remember."

"What's his problem, anyway?" I asked.

"Dmitry's a good kid at heart. He's just been through a lot."

"Well so have I, so has Anton, and so have you for that matter!" I felt the anger building up again.

"What happened to you two, how did you end up here?"

"It's a bizarre story. Unbelievable really." Liza turned on the machine.

"It can't be any more bizarre than our story. Try me," I said.

"OK, here goes. We left for school one morning, and when we got home that afternoon, they were gone. My mother, my father, even the dog was gone. The apartment was empty. We waited for days. When we got hungry enough, we stole a loaf of bread and got caught. At first, the police said they were going to turn us over to the juvenile authorities. But I guess, once they learned what had happened they felt sorry for us. So they turned us over to the Government Division of Child Protection and here we are."

"Did they ever find your parents?" I asked.

"Nope. How about you and Anton? What's your story?"

I told her the condensed version. Mama died. Papa beat up Irina. Papa threw us away, and here we were, too.

"What about your sister?" Liza asked.

"Irina got better and ran away with her boyfriend. She said she couldn't take it here.

"Listen, Liza. I understand how Dmitry could be upset but why the attitude. Why try to fight me?"

"When we first got here, he was beaten on a daily basis by the other kids. And for no good reason that I know of. They were just plain mean.

I tried to help, but they would hold me back. There were too many. I couldn't break free. Eventually, Dmitry accepted hate and fear as a way of life. He learned to be a bully instead of a victim. I should have been able to protect him. I couldn't.

"I know Dmitry's a good person. He shows me all the time. To the rest of the world, he's just an ass."

"I guess I'd have to agree with you there," I said. Liza gave me a look that said *back off*.

"If I don't fight Dmitry, daily beatings will be all Anton, and I can look forward to. Even if I didn't care about me, I wouldn't let that happen to Anton," I told her.

"What about the staff during these beatings? Didn't they do anything?" I asked.

"Oh, sure, they took bets! They didn't care, still, don't." Liza sounded bitter.

"Maybe I can talk to Dmitry before the fight. I'll tell him we're not so different. If we're gonna survive this place, we should stick together not fight each other. Think he might listen?"

"Not before the fight. Maybe after you win," Liza smiled.

I chuckled, "Don't worry. I'll be easy on him."

"I wouldn't be so sassy if I were you. Like I

said, Dmitry's a pretty good fighter. He's been at it for a while, now!"

"I know, Liza," I said.

My stomach had butterflies just thinking about it.

CHAPTER 12

The Fight

When we had finished school for the day, I walked out with Misha. We headed towards the prearranged location for the fight. Liza wasn't sure if she wanted to be there to see her brother and her friend lock horns. We went ahead without her.

We followed the long driveway that led to the back of the property. There sat the ruins of the old garage. The remains should have been torn down long ago. There was no roof, only stone walls covered with vines and weeds. The inside was nothing but rotting floors. It once had held half a dozen bays where the company trucks were repaired and housed.

There was a platform in front of the two center bays. It held gas pumps for refueling. They had rusted through long ago as had the tanks below that housed the gas. They were roped off with orange triangular flags hanging on ropes.

There were more kids than I had expected to come. There were about thirty or so. Word of the fight had gotten around, which wasn't good. The more kids that showed up, the higher were our chances of getting caught.

I was shaking in my boots. I wanted to turn around and go back, but that would have marked me as a coward. Dmitry wouldn't be the only bully at the orphanage who would declare open season on me.

I saw Anton. He was standing right in front of the crowd that had gathered. I approached him.

"Anton, you need to leave, now! This thing is getting out of hand. It's not just between Dmitry and me anymore. All this commotion can't go unnoticed."

"I'm staying," he said stubbornly.

"Damn it, Anton!"

"Having second thoughts, Alex? No one would blame you for running away. You're outclassed, and you know it." Dmitry laughed and turned full circle to take in the reaction of the crowd. He held his arms above his head, fists clenched.

"Listen, Dmitry; we need to do this some other time. You know there are too many people here, we're going to get busted."

He stepped in closer. His eyes squinted. His

teeth clenched.

"We fight here and now or you pull out, and I win." He stepped back and waited for my reaction.

My mouth became dry, and I licked my lips. I looked over at Anton. There was no way out.

"Fine. Let's fight!"

I took off my jacket and slammed it to the ground. The crowd cheered and stepped back.

Dmitry and I faced each other, circling slowly. Each of us waiting for the other to make the first move.

I remembered what Papa said about fighting. *The first one to throw a punch will lose, nearly every time.* So I tried to be patient, circling, waiting, staring him down. It worked. He became impatient and took a swing at me. I ducked, and he missed. I returned with a right hand that landed on his cheek.

More circling.

He landed a good one on my nose, and it started bleeding.

After more circling, I returned with a left to his head. It opened a cut above his eye. Now, he was bleeding.

He stopped, touched the cut, and shook his head. He glared at me, his lips tightly closed. He came at me so fast and hard, all I could do was grab him. I held him in a bear hug to keep him from thrashing me. His sweaty heaving body slipped from my grasp.

As he managed to break free, I pushed him…hard!

He staggered back several feet. Without a sound, the earth beneath him gave way. We all froze as Dmitry disappeared beneath the ground into one of the old gas tanks.

I ran forward to find him hanging onto a tree root. There was a span of about five feet of earth between the ground and the tank. The root he held was about halfway down and looked too flimsy to hold his weight for very long. His legs were hanging into the rotted tank. It was too dark to tell exactly how deep it was.

The fumes from the old gasoline were nearly overpowering. My eyes were burning. It was hard to breathe.

I could hear screams in the background, and someone was yelling for everyone to scatter.

I reached into the hole and grabbed onto

Dmitry's wrist. "Someone help!" I screamed.

Anton and Misha were at my side in an instant.

Their arms weren't long enough to reach Dmitry. I could feel him slipping from my grasp.

"Dmitry, reach up, grab my hand! Hurry!"

It was Liza. She just appeared with Natalia from out of nowhere.

Dmitry stretched up with his free hand. He couldn't reach her. Liza leaned in so far; I was afraid she was about to plummet head first.

"Anton, Misha, grab her legs! Don't let her fall in!" I screamed.

At last, Dmitry got hold of her hand. We pulled and pulled. Anton and Misha were helping Liza. Natalia was helping me. Finally, he was out. We continued to drag him a few more feet away.

Once he was safe, we all collapsed. We were choking and gasping for air. After a while, I could finally breathe. But I was still a little light-headed.

"Everyone ok?" I managed to say.

They all answered, *yes*.

Mr. Evanko came running up with Janko and

two other workers.

"What's going on here!" shouted Mr. Evanko.

He pulled Anton and Misha up by the backs of their shirts, still coughing.

"Who's fighting, here?" yelled Janko.

We stood up. I looked at Dmitry. He said nothing.

"From the looks of you two, it's obvious. You'll pay for this one, smart ass." Janko smiled at me.

"Fighting is against the rules. You know what that means? You ignore the rules, and you pay the consequences. You've been warned before," said Mr. Evanko.

"No one was fighting," I said. "We were just walking, and Dmitry fell into the hole."

"Not fighting, huh?" Mr. Evanko glared at me then at Dmitry.

"Just walking? Why were you just walking all the way back here?"

Dmitry spoke, "I was showing Alex the blown out garage from the revolution. He'd never seen it. He didn't even know it was here."

Mr. Evanko looked at me, "Just sightseeing, Alex? How did you get that nose?"

My first instinct was to come back with something flippant, like "I was born with it." Hahaha. One look at him, and I knew better.

"I must have hit it when I leaned over the hole," I told him. "Or maybe when we were pulling Dmitry up, someone accidentally bumped it."

He looked over at Dmitry. "And you? What happened to your eye?"

"Well, I am the one who fell in, so…" he shrugged.

Janko turned to Liza, Anton, Misha, and Natalia. "What are the four of you doing here?"

"Nothing."

"Walking."

"Tagging along.

"Just looking."

They all answered together in a mumble.

"Enough!" yelled Mr. Evanko. "Back to your dorms. Clean up and stay there. There will be no supper for you tonight!"

We left immediately and ran back to the school. When we got inside the building, we looked to be sure no one else was around. We burst out laughing.

"That was so close," said Anton.

"Do you think he believed us?" I asked.

"Not on your life. It's just late in the day, and he wants to go home, not deal with us," said Misha.

We reached the stairs and were walking up.

"I don't know about that," said Liza, "I think they all love it when we turn against one another. He probably hopes you two jackasses will continue the fight. When you've hurt each other enough, he and his faculty of goons will step in and finish the job."

We stopped at the second-floor landing.

"So," I said, "if we finish this, we'll be doing exactly what they want us to do?"

"Exactly what they want you to do," repeated Liza.

"Dmitry, I don't know about you, but I'm not ready to play right into their hands, are you?" I asked him. "I say screw 'em. Let's end this, shake hands and move on. What do you think?"

"I think I smell a chicken, a big, rotten chicken." He smiled that nasty smile of his, crossed his arms, and leaned against the wall.

"Dmitry!" shouted Liza. "Will you think straight for just one minute? We've been providing entertainment for them with our petty fights for long enough. When are we going to stand up and start helping instead of hurting each other? No one is going to help us but us."

He thought for a minute and then he held out his hand. I took it, and we began our shaky truce.

He turned and walked down the hall towards our dorm. "Besides, it's pretty obvious I already won."

I followed. "What do you mean? I was slaughtering you so bad; you had to jump into a hole to get away."

"I jumped in that hole to keep from destroying you. Killing is against the rules too, you know."

"And, you're welcome by the way," I told him.

"For what?"

"Saving your life, you ungrateful—"

"I was just climbing out on my own. I didn't need your help."

"Alex, Dmitry!" yelled Liza.

We turned. Her face was red, and the vein in her forehead was bulging. I swore I saw smoke coming out of her ears.

Dmitry and I looked at each other. Then he put an arm around my shoulder. I did the same to him. We turned and walked down the hall.

"Good fight, Alex, old boy. Oh, and thanks for saving my life."

"Not a problem, buddy. You sure had me in a vice. Good thing you fell in that hole."

***

We lay in our beds, waiting for Janko to come in and wreak havoc. When he didn't, I decided to read. I hadn't read my comics since before we arrived. I went to my cube, got my box, and reached in, to the bottom where I had hidden them. I felt nothing. I pulled out the box and dumped it out on the floor. They were gone! My precious comics, gone!

"What are you looking for?" asked Dmitry.

"My comic books. They're not...did you take them?" I asked slowly, trying to control the rage I was feeling.

"Not me. It was Janko. He took those weeks ago. Sorry, Alex, I thought you knew."

"Janko? Why would he take them?"

"He takes whatever he wants. They all do."

"I thought I had them hidden," I said. There was no way I could get them back from Janko. I had to come to terms with the fact they were gone forever.

I went back to my bed. I lay there staring at the ceiling. Dmitry went over, packed up my things and returned the box to its cube.

When the guys came in Dmitry steered them away from me.

After a while, Janko came in to shut the lights off. I couldn't even look his way.

When the lights went out, I lay in the dark, thinking. Thinking about how we got here. How Irina left us. All the changes we'd gone through, and how much we had lost in the process.

Sure, the comics weren't the biggest thing I had ever lost. Somehow losing them just broke my spirit. For the first time in a very long time, I felt hot tears burning my cheeks. Then, the dam broke. I stifled my sobs in my pillow. I couldn't stop. I felt the life inside was leaving me. I drifted into a fitful sleep.

I woke up the next morning, before sunrise. I had no way of knowing what time it was, only that it was still dark. My head hurt. I was thirsty. But I didn't feel broken anymore. I cried it out of me. I had to remember, no matter how bad things got around here, we wouldn't be in this place forever. Anton and I would have a life one day. I thought of Dmitry and how protective he had been when he knew I was in a bad way. Could we end up being friends, after all?

I got up and went into the bathroom to take a shower. By the time I finished, the dorm was up and getting ready for the day.

"How's it going?" asked Dmitry.

"Never better," I answered honestly. "I'm starving. What do you say we clean up and get some breakfast?"

"Give me five minutes," answered Dmitry.

CHAPTER 13

The Holidays

Over the next few weeks, Dmitry and I got along pretty well. Liza was happy our feud was over. We spent all our free time together, along with Misha, Anton, and Natalia.

Anton made a new friend. Her name was Anna. She was seven years old. They were in the same class.

Anna was a sweet, frightened, little girl. Anton became her protector after he called off a couple of girls in the hall. They were threatening her the first day she arrived. He was very fond of her, like a little sister. She followed him like a timid puppy.

Anna's mother had abandoned her at the market. She told her to wait next to the bread and left her there. At closing time Anna went outside, still waiting for her mother to return to her. As he was leaving for home, the merchant noticed her sitting in the cold. She was scared and crying. He called the authorities. Poor Anna wasn't as lucky as we had been. When none of her family could be found, she landed in an abusive home. Probably worse than here, at least for her. Eventually, she came to the boarding school.

She arrived the day Dmitry and I fought, about a month ago. Another kid who was just thrown away. There were so many of us here.

One morning, we all met for breakfast as usual. The holidays were not that far away. The New Year was just twelve days away and a week after that came Christmas. Christmas day was on January seventh, but the festivities continued the entire week of January seventh to the fourteenth. We were lucky to get one day at our house after Mama died. But, most people spent the entire week dressing up, visiting homes, and singing Christmas songs. There were lots of blessings and lots of exceptional food. Puppet shows of the Nativity, holiday concerts, and Christmas fairs were everywhere.

I asked Liza and Dmitry what we would do for the holidays.

"It's actually not bad," said Liza. "The reporters come to take pictures and videos to show the people of Luhansk how wonderfully their orphans are treated. The staff lines up with us, and we all smile for the camera because we're so well treated and happy here! If they ask us questions, we always say how lucky we are to be here in this wonderful school, *or else!*"

She covered her face like Dracula and let out a hideous laugh.

"For real?" asked Anton.

"Yup," said Dmitry. "For real. We decorate a tree, and we get small gifts. A piece of candy or sometimes a little toy for the primary kids. It's the only time all year they have to be nice to us. You can't have the cameras showing black eyes and swollen lips."

"Maybe we can make decorations," said Anna. It was the first time I saw her smile.

"Sure," said Liza, "we can gather some holly and make wreaths."

"We'll all go outside after school to get stuff," said Anton.

"Not yet. We can't start too early. The supervisory units don't allow decorations until after the New Year. Christmas is on a Monday this year, so we can probably decorate the week before," Natalia declared.

We had to cut it short. It was time to go to school. We left the dining room and passed through the living area. Most of the staff were sitting in front of the television. The caption on the screen read 'Special Report.' We stopped to listen. There was no use rushing to school when all the teachers and most of the workers were all here, in front of the television.

The reporter was a man, middle-aged, with dark hair. The screen was black and white, so it was impossible to know his actual hair color. He said that he was reporting from the capital city of Kharvisk.

"For those of you who are just tuning in; the president of Ekrunia, Bohdan Ebuchowski, has just left the podium. He announced the end of subsidies for all workers beginning the first of the year. This will include everyone working in coal, copper, and iron ore, as well as the sandstone, limestone, chalk, and marlstone industries. This cutback comes after months of debate and threats on both sides of the issue."

Mr. Kovalski stood and said, "We had better begin school." And he left.

We all walked over to the school. When class started, Mr. Kovalski opened with a discussion of the news.

"I know you have questions," he began. "First, let me refresh your memories. As you will recall, after the people's revolution, the government took over all industries that have to do with natural resources, coal, gas, iron, and so on. Labor agreed to work for meager wages, as long as subsidies were paid in addition to regular wages. It was supposed to be a temporary solution to a national money crisis.

"Now after all these years, the government is not only failing to give the wages it promised—it is taking away the only means the workers have to live, the subsidies. Without the extra money, many families will starve, even go homeless. The workers can't accept this," he concluded.

"What can they do about it?" asked Nazar.

"That's an excellent question. What indeed.

"Well, nothing that wouldn't create a response from the government. The first thing they would probably do is to strike. That could shut down most of the country. The refineries, construction, metal foundries, all would eventually come to a standstill without the natural resources the mines and drilling provide. The government won't stand for that."

"Then what's going to happen?" asked Liza.

"My guess would be nothing, until after the holidays. Then, if talks don't resume—well, we'll just have to wait and see."

***

It was Sunday, December 31st, New Year's Eve. Everyone spent most of the day gathering greens and berries for wreaths and decorations. When we came in for supper, it seemed like most of the staff was already celebrating. They were in excellent spirits and a lot louder than usual.

Anton and I filled our trays with fried potato cakes, cabbage rolls filled with rice, and bread. When we sat down at the table, Dmitry leaned over and said, "The supervisory units are sipping vodka out of their coffee cups!"

"Happy New Year!" Anton said with a slur. Everyone laughed.

"Tomorrow we get to decorate the Christmas tree!" Anna said. She was excited. "Do we have all the stuff we need to make decorations after supper?"

"We collected tons of stuff today!" said Liza. "The staff has everything set up in the common room. There's string, tape, paper for pictures, and wire to make hooks. They want the orphanage to look its best for the reporters and politicians."

We finished supper, cleaned up, and went to the common room for Christmas crafts. Just as Liza said, everything was there for us. We gathered some supplies and found a table.

Anna and Anton sat together making a wreath. It wasn't staying together very well. But they were laughing about it and having fun. Liza offered to help. They thanked her and said they wanted to make it by themselves.

Suddenly we heard fireworks. We ran to the windows. We could see the spray of color in the night sky. We stood quietly as we watched. Some of us remembered past holidays with family.

"My mother took me to see the fireworks once," said Anna. "I remember it was so loud. I was scared."

"The first time I saw fireworks, they scared me too," said Misha.

"Hey, Alex. Remember the time you, me, and Papa all climbed up on the roof to watch fireworks? He was so drunk, he couldn't get back on the ladder to get down," smiled Anton.

"So what happened? How did you get him down?" asked Natalia.

Anton and I looked at each other remembering. We started to laugh.

"We didn't. We left him up there, and he fell asleep. He nearly froze," I said.

"Boy was he mad when he made it down! It was the middle of the night, and we were in bed sleeping. He burst into our room, yelling, 'What kind of sons are you? You just leave your father to die in the cold? What if I had rolled off the roof?' He was blue, and shaking like a scared baby!" laughed Anton.

"Then he made Irina get up to make him a pot of hot coffee. He sweetened it with more vodka. She was madder at us that he was!"

That was the first time we had talked about Irina since the day we came here.

I leaned in closer to Anton and asked him, quietly, "Do you ever think about her?"

"Sure, sometimes. I like to think she's happy with Paul. They have a nice house, and they never ever fight." he smiled.

The evening just flew by. Soon it was time to go to the dorms and go to bed. We all said good night and Happy New Year.

Dmitry and Misha were acting funny. I asked them what was up. They pulled out a bottle of juice.

"Vodka," said Misha.

"Are you crazy?" I asked. "If Janko catches you

with that he'll make mincemeat out of both of you!"

Dmitry took the bottle and hid it under his pillow.

"Quick, let's get to bed before he gets here," he said.

Sure enough. Janko showed up for lights out fifteen minutes early. I guess he was in a hurry to get to the party in the staff's living quarters.

When it was clear, all the boys got up quietly. Dmitry and Misha weren't the only one to steal and sneak contraband into the dorm. We were about to have a New Year's party of our own!

By midnight half the dorm was in the bathroom throwing up, including Dmitry and Misha. The rest were passed out or talking in groups on the floor. It wasn't the first time I'd tasted vodka. There was enough of it in our house, thanks to Papa. But I decided long ago I would never end up like him. So I barely tasted any. Besides, the first time I tried some I got so sick I thought I was gonna die! That was enough vodka for me.

At breakfast the next morning, some of the boys from the secondary dorm were missing. Sick, they said. Caught the flu, they said.

Janko was pissed! He knew the flu wasn't going

around. He just couldn't prove that it was an unauthorized New Year's party gone wrong.

We finished breakfast. Then with the help of the older kids, we set up the tree. They had gone out the day before and cut it down themselves. It was about ten feet tall, very full, and very heavy. When they finished putting on the lights, we decorated the tree with berries and paper chain garland. Then we hung the some of the wreaths we had made, on the walls. We stepped back and admired our work.

The rest of the week was business as usual. School, work, and Janko's sour mood. It was hard for him to keep his fists to himself. But he had his orders. No marks for the pictures.

Soon it was Christmas morning. We got to sleep in as late as we wanted to, as long as we were dressed in our best clothes and reported to the common rooms by noon.

I met Anton on the landing. When we got upstairs, we were surprised to see how festive it was! The tree lights were on, and Christmas music was playing. The rest of our wreaths were being used as centerpieces and had been placed on tables that were covered with crisp white tablecloths. A special loaf of bread called a *Kolach* was put on each of the tables with a lighted beeswax candle set in the center. This tradition was to remind us of the

Star of Bethlehem. There were napkins and eating utensils at every seat.

Most of our guests had already arrived and were seated at a long table in the front of the dining room with Mr. Evanko. It was designated as a place of honor. To the left and right of the head table were two more tables. They were for Mr. Evanko's staff, the dorm supervisors, and the teachers.

All the kids were mingling about, some staring around the rooms in awe. Many of us had never seen the dining, and common rooms look anything but sad and gloomy.

The kitchen staff had prepared a traditional dinner of *holubtsi*, stuffed cabbage rolls, *vushka,* small dumplings with mushrooms*, borscht*, beet soup, and *kutia*, the same sweet pudding that Sophia had made for us.

Before the kitchen staff served the meal, the seventh and eighth graders were brought up to the front of the dining room, to sing some Christmas songs for the reporters and politicians. We practiced for weeks before Christmas. Our first song was *'Boh predvičnyj narodilsja'* (God Eternal is Born). At first, everyone just listened. Then, they all joined in.

Our second song was *'Nebo i zemlia nyni*

torzhestvuiut' (Heaven and Earth Rejoice Today). It was a refrain, and we sang it as a round. Each table chose a verse and joined in. The entire room was singing.

When we finished, it was time for the young kids. They sang and again everyone sang along. I had to admit; they were cute. Our guests gave them a real show of appreciation. We ended our entertainment with a special blessing. Then it was time to sit and enjoy our feast!

We were allowed to sit in our usual places. But we didn't have to stand in line for our food. Dishes were served at the tables.

We had been told not to begin eating until Mr. Evanko gave another blessing. We sat with our hands in our laps and waited.

"Do you think these people are dumb enough to believe that this is how they really treat us all the time?" Dmitry asked under his breath.

"Who cares? Just shut up and enjoy it," said Liza, "Christmas only comes once a year!"

"Yeah, and we'll pay for it the rest of the year," added Misha.

Mr. Evanko stood and tapped a spoon on his glass to get our attention. He began by thanking everyone for visiting our humble boarding school.

As he spoke, the two photographers snapped pictures of him, the politicians, the staff, teachers, and of course the cheerful faces of the sweet orphans who lived here.

He thanked us for singing. Thanked the kitchen staff for preparing such a delicious meal. Thanked everyone for working so hard all year and on and on, and yadda, yadda, yadda.

"I'm starving!" whispered Anton, "And the food's gonna get cold!"

Finally…"and may you be blessed in many ways. *Z Rizdvom!* (Merry Christmas!) Enjoy your meal."

The room was dead silent as we dug into our feast. (No time to talk with all this delicious food to eat.) We had just about finished our meal and were ready for dessert when we had a surprise visitor. In walked Grandfather Frost (our Santa) and his granddaughter Snowflake to deliver gifts!

Grandfather told us the legend of the spiders, just as Mama had when I was small.

"One family in the village was too poor to have a decorated Christmas tree in their house. The mother had hung a few meager nuts and fruits on

the small tree outside their door in hopes of bringing some cheer to her children's' Christmas Day celebration.

"On Christmas Eve, the spiders heard her prayers and hung their webs all over the tree. As the sun came up, its rays glittered and sparkled on the dew that was sprinkled on the webs and turned them into silver and gold."

When he finished, Snowflake gave everyone a small spider made of beads and a piece of candy.

After our guests left, we spent the afternoon playing games, and just being happy. I thought of Irina. Even though part of me was still angry with her for running out on us, I hoped she was enjoying this day as much as I was.

As if reading my mind, Anton came over and asked, "Do you think Irina is having a good Christmas?"

I smiled. "Yes. And the answer to your next question little brother is yes. She misses us, too."

***

When we got back to the dorm that night, I walked over to my bed and saw a package sitting on my pillow. I looked around and caught Dmitry watching me. He hastily looked away. I picked up the package and opened it. Inside the box were my comics! I looked over at him. He was smiling.

"How did you…"

"Trade secret," he said. "*Z Rizdvom!* (Merry Christmas!), Alex. Be sure to hide them better than you did the first time."

I couldn't believe Dmitry would do that for me. I would never forget it.

Chapter 14

Bad Politics

The Christmas holiday lasted another week, but not at the Luhansk Boarding School for Orphans. The teachers had gone on holiday, so we had no school the rest of that week. But the work schedule doubled up. All the decorations had to be taken down, as did the tree. The kitchen crew would be cleaning up from the festivities along with their daily duties. And in the laundry, all the linens from Christmas had to be washed and ironed before they were returned to the rental warehouse, downtown.

Monday, the day after our Christmas celebration, our regular schedule went back into effect. I got up at seven, washed up, and got dressed. The dorm was already empty, except for Dmitry. He was waiting for me to go to breakfast with him. We were going to meet up with the others in the dining room.

Just as we were about to walk out the door, Janko came in and blocked our way.

"We were just leaving," said Dmitry, thinking as I did, that Janko was there to hurry us along.

But, when he tried to step around Janko, Dmitry got a fist in his stomach. He doubled over and went down to his knees.

I shouted, "What the hell did you do that for?" I bent to help Dmitry to his feet.

Before I knew it, Janko grabbed me by the throat and slammed me up against the wall. As I attempted to struggle, his hold on my neck tightened. I could hardly breathe.

"I seem to be missing something from my room. My gut tells me you and your little girlfriend here have something to do with its disappearance. Time to fess up, smartass."

He released his grip. I bent over, trying to catch my breath.

"We don't know what you're talking about," said Dmitry, who was struggling to stand.

Janko backhanded him and split his lip.

"No... now I think you do." He spoke slowly and calculatingly. "Although, how you got into my locked room and stole my property is still a mystery. In fact, I can't figure out how you managed to get into the staff quarters without being seen. You can both fill me in later. Right now I want you to return my property."

I stood up and looked him in the eye. "We don't have your property," I sneered.

Another backhand. This time it was aimed at me. Janko's ring caught me just above the eye and opened a cut on my brow. I was knocked to the floor. Blood ran into my eye and down my cheek.

Janko grabbed Dmitry and threw him down between the rows of neatly made beds. He kicked Dmitry in the stomach, then walked over to the door. Janko took out his keys and locked it. He tore through the room looking for the comics.

He ripped every bed apart. He tossed all the boxes from the shelves and threw mattresses on the floor. He even hit the bathroom and checked toilet tanks! When he was convinced they weren't in the dorm, he walked back to where we were leaning.

"I know you have them." Janko stared at us. His face was contorted with hate and anger.

"Clean this up! And don't think this is the end of it. I will get my comics back."

"You mean my comics," I muttered. I glared at him. I didn't care if he hit me again.

Finally, Janko sauntered over to the door, unlocked it, and left.

"Are you OK?" I asked Dmitry.

"I think I'm going to be sick." He ran into the bathroom.

When he got back to the room, I had already started picking up the mattresses and bedding.

"OK, where are they?" Dmitry asked.

I smiled and walked over to the air duct in the ceiling above a bed halfway down the row. I climbed onto the headboard and touched the vent cover.

"I'll be damned!" Dmitry smiled then grimaced. He touched his split lip, it was swollen twice its size, and looked painful.

I jumped down. My eye started bleeding again. I lifted my shirt and pressed it against the cut.

When we didn't show up for breakfast, Liza and Misha came looking for us. As she was sneaking into the boys' dorm, she saw blood.

"Oh my God! What happened?" Liza shouted as she ran over to Dmitry. She looked over at me. "You're both bleeding! We have to get you a doctor!" Misha ran in behind her.

"Get out of here, Liza!" Dmitry yelled back. "Do you know what they'll do to you if they catch you in the boys' dorm?"

She ignored his question. "Did you two fight?" she asked.

"No!" we both yelled in unison.

"Then what happened?"

"OK," I said. "It was Janko. Now get out. You're already late for work. If they come looking for you…"

"Are you sure you'll be alright? Maybe I should go and get Mrs. Galey."

"Listen to me, Liza. Don't make things worse. We have to get this cleaned up before Janko comes back to check. Please, if you want to help just leave us, now."

I turned to Misha. "You too, Misha. Go, please."

After they left, we managed to clean up the dorm, with a few exceptions. We had bled on several of the sheets.

"You rest a minute, and I'll get clean sheets," I told Dmitry.

I went downstairs to the linen closet, got the sheets, and returned to the dorm. When I got back Mr. Misko, the custodian (Dmitry's boss,) was there.

"What's up?" I asked Dmitry.

"You boys never showed up for work. Mr. Chorney reported you." Mr. Misko answered for him.

Mr. Misko was one of the good guys. He figured we would be together. So he came to warn us.

"Finish and get to work. Hurry," he said as he left.

***

When I walked into the laundry, everyone

stopped to look. I didn't have time to clean myself up. I just threw on another shirt and hurried there. Mr. Chorney came over. I turned my face away. He reached over and turned my face towards him.

"Well, Mr. Krisko, run into a wall?"

"Something like that, sir," I answered.

"Hmm." He grunted. "Get to work and don't bleed on the clean clothes."

***

We broke for lunch. Liza and I grabbed a couple of trays and got on the serving line. Everywhere I looked someone was staring. The cooks were no exception. Because no one knew what had happened, no one dared say a word.

We went to the table. Anton turned white when he saw me.

"I'm fine," I said quickly.

Dmitry came in. The entire scene repeated itself.

"Hard to believe this is the same place we celebrated Christmas," said Natalia.

We were all pretty quiet during lunch. Dmitry was having a hard time eating. His lip was swollen and sore. He finally threw down his fork and gave up.

I wasn't very hungry. My head was hurting, and

I was feeling a little queasy. I looked up and saw Janko coming towards us.

Dmitry leaned over, "What, now?"

"I don't know, but I'm sure we won't like it," I replied.

"You two, report to Mr. Evanko's office. He's requested your delightful presence. Pronto, move it!" Janko sounded pleased. That could only mean more trouble.

"Relax," he replied, "I didn't tell him anything. If you have the need to confess your little indiscretion do feel free. I'm sure Mr. Evanko would be very interested."

***

Mr. Evanko's office door was open. I knocked gently. He looked up from his reading and did a double take. He motioned for us to sit. He leaned back in his chair and crossed his arms. He continued to glare at us.

After an eternity, he spoke. "I hope you boys didn't decide to finish your fight after all."

"No sir, we didn't fight. We just had a little accident," I said. Dmitry was looking down at his hands.

"If you say so. But it looks to me, as though you ran into the wrong end of a big fist." He was laughing.

"Well, down to business so that I can resume my holiday. I have a job for you two boys. I have…I mean the school has made a deal with the linen rental warehouse in town. We'll be supplying some of their laundry needs. Beginning today, you two will be responsible for daily pickup and delivery. These deliveries will be in addition to your other responsibilities, of course."

"You mean go into town?" I asked.

Dmitry wasn't looking down at his hands anymore.

Mr. Evanko gave me a mocking smile. "Well, Mr. Janko was right to recommend you for the job. You're as sharp as a tack!"

"How do we get there?" I asked.

"Walk. It's only a few miles each way."

Dmitry and I looked at each other baffled. Did we hear this right?

"Why us? Shouldn't one of the workers go?" Dmitry finally spoke.

"It's simply a question of bad politics," he said.

"I don't know if you're aware, but things in and around town have become a bit, shall I say, chaotic. Protests are going on. No one expected that they would begin during Christmas week, but the people are extremely upset over the voucher cuts. I can't say I blame them. But, I wouldn't want to risk one of my valuable employees getting injured. They won't hurt you. You're just children.

"Now, if you're thinking that this would be the perfect opportunity just to keep going, let me remind you that you. Dmitry, you have a sister here, and you, Alex have a brother. If you do anything foolish, be assured, your siblings will have to pay the price. And a hefty price it will be."

"If there aren't any questions, report to Mr. Chorney in the laundry. He will give you all the details."

He went back to his reading and ignored us. We rose to leave.

Apparently, there were still no questions!

***

Mr. Chorney was waiting for us in the laundry. "Come into my office," he told us.

I looked over at Liza. I could tell she was dying to know what was going on. Dmitry gave her a 'thumbs up,' and we both smiled at her before going into the office. She looked more confused than before. Mr. Chorney closed the door behind us.

He explained that we would leave every day at ten, after school. We were to walk to the linen warehouse carrying the clean laundry, drop it off, and pick up the dirty laundry.

"You'll be back by one thirty at the latest. One

o'clock, if you care to eat lunch. You were supposed to start today, but I just spoke to Mr. Evanko. I explained that we are behind in our work. I didn't tell him it was because you didn't show up this morning. I probably should have. He wasn't happy about starting a day late. But he agreed to begin the program tomorrow. That's it. Both of you go to work."

Dmitry left to find Mr. Misko for his daily assignment. I dreaded going back to the laundry room. I knew Liza was going to bombard me with questions. She did.

"We'll talk later at supper, and I'll tell you everything. We need to get this laundry done," I assured Liza.

***

The dining room was buzzing with news of the protests.

"I'm afraid you'll get hurt again if you go to town. Look at your head. You should have stitches," said Anton.

"It's not like they have a choice," said Natalia.

"It might be a nice break," said Dmitry.

"You wouldn't run away without us, would you?" asked Liza. "I don't know what we'd do without you two."

"Of course not!" answered Dmitry. "Besides,

we gave our word that we'd be back every day by one."

"Or what?" asked Liza.

"Or nothing!" I said. "Let's clean up and play drunkard. I've had enough questions for one day."

CHAPTER 15

The Protest

There wasn't any school the next morning. We went straight to work after breakfast. Dmitry met me at the laundry at ten o'clock, and we packed all the clean linens into one of the laundry trucks. It was a canvas basket thirty inches long, twenty inches wide, and twenty inches high. It had a handle at each end. Usually, it would be mounted on wheels or a cart. But wheels would be impossible to maneuver on our route. Dmitry and I had to carry it.

Pervaiske was a small city, about forty square miles. The warehouse was about four miles away on the far side of the town. There was one road going back and forth, but it was old and mostly deserted. It was much shorter to go in a straight line from just south of the orphanage. It was pretty flat and mostly open. We followed the railroad tracks for about a quarter of a mile south. Then we went straight west through the overgrown ruins of what was once a neighborhood.

There were no streets left, and most of the houses were gone. Some of the foundations remained with the cellars beneath. They were overgrown with fauna and blended into the woods that surrounded them. Some places had the remains of walls covered in vines.

We stopped to rest for a minute. We were getting blisters on our hands from the weight of the basket.

"Can you imagine this as a real neighborhood with kids playing outside?" asked Dmitry.

"No. But I can imagine us missing lunch if we don't get moving. Let's go."

We kept our course. We planned to intersect with Kuibyshanka Street. It was the main street and went through town to the linen warehouse. Before we reached the intersection, we passed close to the neighborhood where Irina, Anton, and I grew up. My house, my old house, was just a few blocks in. I wondered if Papa was home. I thought of Mrs. Babich and of that night when our lives changed forever.

"Hey, where'd you go?" Dmitry's voice brought me back to the present.

"I'm right here."

"Your body is, but your mind was a thousand miles away. What were you thinking about?" he asked.

"We used to live right down the street with my father…before," I answered.

"Think he's there?"

"If he is," I said, "he's probably passed out drunk already."

"So— does that mean you don't want to *pop in* for a hug?" Dmitry and his unceasing sarcasm.

"Keep it up, and I'll be *poppin'* the other side of that fat lip of yours!"

"Whoaaaaaa!! I'm so scared! Mercy Master, please!" He held his free hand over his heart as if begging.

"Haha. You are so funny, Dmitry! You just kill me," I said.

Finally, we made it to the warehouse. We walked through the front door. Inside was a reception area with chairs and a book rack full of old magazines. On the walls were pictures of freshly made hospital beds and beautifully set tables. All of them highlighting the linens available for rent.

Directly across from the front door was a receptionist, sitting at a desk. Behind her was a price list of all their available products. There was a man, about thirty, sitting on her desk. She was laughing at something he had said. He was dressed in a dark gray suit, a white shirt, and a gray and white striped tie. They both turned and looked at us as we entered.

"Back to work," he said as he stood. He was tall, medium build. He had neatly trimmed hair and was cleanly shaven. The receptionist smiled at him and watched him as he walked through a door beside her desk.

When the door opened, we could see the busy laundry room at the end of the long hallway. Glass doors separated the two.

The receptionist turned and looked us up and down. Her nose wrinkled as if she smelled something rotten, and her eyebrows were in a frown.

"Do you want something?" she barked. I think she was angry that we interrupted her and the man in the suit.

"We're here to deliver the laundry from Luhansk Boarding School," Dmitry responded.

"Not here you're not! Go around back to the service entrance. You're not allowed in the office area."

"Can't we go right through that door?" I asked.

"Nooo, you can go right through *that* door," she said while pointing to the front entrance.

"Then you can go around back to the service entrance as I told you."

Dmitry glared for a moment, and then he smiled. *Damn,* I thought, *here we go.* I immediately walked over to the door and opened it. Dmitry held on to the canvas basket, stood his ground, and stopped me in my tracks. Unless I dropped my end of the basket, I could only wait.

Still smiling and with an exaggerated wave of his arm, he bowed from the waist.

"Forgive us milady. For we have soiled this hallowed ground on which you walk. We should have known that trash like us should never enter by the front door. Please forgive us." Dmitry began backing his way to the door, bowing over and over.

"So very sorry… never again…we beg for your forgiveness…"

As he reached the door, he turned to me with a look of agony.

"My God, man, we have contaminated the very air that milady breathes!" he wailed.

At this point, I yanked on the basket and pulled him outside. I smiled and shrugged at the receptionist. She looked at us with loathing.

"What're you trying to prove?" I asked.

"Did you see the way she looked at us?" he shouted.

"Have you seen the way we look? We're cut, bruised, and swollen. Not to mention sweaty and dusty from our little four-mile stroll. Damn, Dmitry!"

I started walking towards the back of the building. Dmitry was silent, but only for a minute.

"Yeah, I can see how she might have been taken aback. You do look pretty Frankenstein'ish. I probably should have walked in front—you know kinda hiding you."

"Dmitry, I swear…"

"A lot, I know. I've been meaning to mention it."

***

The people in the back were much more helpful than the receptionist had been. The guy we saw sitting on her desk was there. He had taken off his jacket and rolled up the sleeves of his dress shirt. As soon as he saw us, he came over and introduced himself.

"Hi, guys. I'm Vika Burick, the plant manager. Are you boys from the orphanage?"

We told him we were.

"Why don't you put that basket down while I show you the ropes? Did you see any protesters on the way in?"

"No, none," Dmitry said.

"Well, you will sooner or later. It's not the regular workers you have to be careful of, nor the muscle the unions sent to back them up. The workers are our people. They come from here, and they're raising their families here. They're angry, but they won't hurt kids.

"It's the police. They're taking their orders from the capital, and president Ebuchowski has ordered them to get the workers back to work at any cost. If they decide to start swinging, they won't care who gets in the way."

I felt confused. Why was he telling us this? Should we be nervous?

He yelled over to one of the men. "Hey, Mike,

got a minute?"

Mike came rushing over. "Sure."

"Boys, I want you to meet Mike. He pretty much keeps things on track around here. Mike, I'd like you to meet…" He looked over for us to give our names.

"Alex."

"Dmitry."

"Alex and Dmitry. They're the boys from the boarding school. They'll be coming every day to pick up and deliver." Mike stared at our injuries but didn't ask questions.

"Nice to meet you, boys. Did you carry that thing all the way here?" he pointed to the basket. "Why isn't it on a cart with wheels? Pulling is much easier than carrying."

"We didn't take the roads. It's faster to come straight across the fields and through the wooded area," I told him.

"So what's your hurry?" he smiled

"We have to be back by one if we want to eat lunch," said Dmitry.

"You mean if you're late they won't feed you?"

Dmitry just shrugged. Mike looked over at Vika.

"It's bad enough Evanko lines his pockets off the backs of these kids. He doesn't feed them if they're late? And he's the one who sent them in the first place. Why are we doing business with a guy like that?"

"I told you, Mike, it's not my call. Maybe we should talk about this later."

Mike nodded.

"When you get here, you're going to bring the cart to station five, over here." Mike led us over.

"Boys, meet Daria. She'll check and count the pieces. Then she'll sign off on your paperwork. Hang on to it. It proves all the pieces were returned. Daria, this is Dmitry and Alex."

"Hi," she said.

"Then over to station two. Here you count the pieces and sign them off here, on this form. You take the copy and leave the original. Bring it back the next day with your delivery so that Daria can check it off. Get it?"

"Got it," I said. Dmitry nodded.

He showed us how to count and mark the paperwork. Everything that they rented was listed, and we had to mark how many of each we were picking up. It was easy, but it took time. Time we hadn't counted on. There would be no way to make it back by one.

Mike must have been thinking the same thing. When we were ready to head back, he handed us two sandwiches from the vending machine and two Cokes.

"Looks like you're gonna be late for lunch. Here. Eat these on the way back."

We thanked him and left.

We walked and ate. It was delicious.

"Did you hear what Mike said about Mr. Evanko lining his pockets?" Dmitry asked.

"Yeah, so he's also a crook. Doesn't surprise me," I responded.

"I wonder if Mr. Chorney's in on it, too."

"Why?" I asked.

"Well, it's his job to run the laundry. If there's more laundry, there's more to take care of. I bet he wouldn't be thrilled to hear all the extra work is making his boss rich and he doesn't even get an extra chunk of coal."

"Oh boy, I see where this is going. If we let it slip to Mr. Chorney and he knows, he'll be pissed. If we let it slip and he doesn't know, he'll be pissed."

"Win, win," said Dmitry.

"We don't need that kind of trouble. Let it go."

"OK. But it would be fun to watch it play out." Dmitry shrugged.

***

We went to the warehouse every day, and every day Mike had a sandwich and a Coke waiting for us. We looked forward to it! He was a great guy. Not soft but kind. Not sweet but caring, in a manly way. Neither Dmitry nor I had anyone like him in our lives. So when we came in with a delivery a couple of weeks into the job, and he asked for a favor, we jumped at the chance to help.

"The guy who picks up the laundry from the hospital is out sick. I could use you to pick up today. It's only about a mile. The problem is, it's over by the courthouse. They're protesting over there today.

I checked, and it's only a peaceful march with signs and slogans. Should be very calm. But if you have any reservations you don't have to go."

"We'll go!" I said.

"Sure no problem," said Dmitry.

We got there in just a few minutes. A basket didn't hinder us, so we made great time.

Sure enough. There were protesters everywhere. Lots of signs and lots of slogans.

The march was ending on the courthouse square but not the protest. People were standing around yelling out slogans and waving their signs up and down. We walked past without incident. A couple of blocks down was the hospital.

Mike told us where to go to pick up the laundry. We went around the back and did all the paperwork Mike had given us. Then picked up the canvas basket (we left the cart we were used to carrying at the warehouse) and headed to the warehouse to drop off the paperwork before going back to the school.

We were less than a block away from the courthouse when we heard a gunshot! People started scattering in all directions. It wasn't clear who fired the first shot, but suddenly the police, who were dressed in full riot gear, aimed their rifles into the crowd. Some managed to get off a shot before, within seconds, protesters were overrunning them. They began beating people off with rifle butts and clubs. People were fighting back with anything they could find, even their signs. The fighting spread out of the square and in what seemed an instant, we were right in the middle! We dropped the basket and ran. Out of the corner of my eye, I saw Dmitry heading right into a group of police officers. They were blindly beating anything that moved. Some had handguns and were shooting into the crowd.

"Dmitry! Dmitry! This way, hurry!" I screamed.

Thankfully, he heard me and changed direction. We started pushing our way through the crowd. We were trying to head away from the square and towards the warehouse. Suddenly, I tripped and landed on top of someone. I lifted myself and looked right into the open eyes of one of the protesters. He didn't move. I screamed involuntarily, a loud piercing sound.

Dmitry stopped and came back to help me. As he bent to pull me up, I saw a figure in black reach up with a club in his hand. I pulled Dmitry down just as the club came down towards his head and missed.

We got on all fours and began crawling through

any gap we saw. I finally saw an opening and yelled for Dmitry to follow.

When we stood to run, I couldn't put any weight on my ankle. Dmitry put his arm around my waist, and I put my arm around his shoulder. He supported me as we broke free of the fighting and ran back towards the warehouse. The rioting hadn't made it that far.

Vika and Mike were out front. When they spotted us coming, they ran to meet us and helped us to the safety of the warehouse.

"You're hurt," said the receptionist. She seemed to be talking to both of us.

"I'm sorry. We lost the pickup from the hospital. There was shooting, and people were screaming and running…"

"Don't worry about it, Alex. It's no big deal," said Vika. "Julia, run out back and get the first aid kit." The receptionist complied.

He helped me over to a chair. My entire body was shaking uncontrollably, and my heart was racing. He quickly checked me for injuries. The cut over my eye had reopened and was bleeding. My ankle had a severe sprain, but it wasn't broken. He gave me a compress for my lip and told me to press hard. Then he turned his attention to Dmitry.

"Mike," Vika called.

Mike came over and looked at Dmitry's hand. "Looks like at least three out of five metacarpals are broken. Who are we going to get to set it? The hospital is out of the question." Vika looked at him.

"I don't know, Vika, it's been awhile, and I was only a medic, not a real doctor," said Mike.

"I've seen your work, Mike. You were more than a medic when we were fighting in the Middle East. You're all we've got right now. Do the best you can, and we'll get him a real doctor tomorrow when things quiet down."

"They're killing people in the streets. Shooting them down like dogs! How can it quiet down?" I shouted.

"For a time it will. Trust me," Mike said calmly.

I looked over at Dmitry. He looked like he was about to pass out.

"Alex, the time. Anton and Liza."

He was right. We were going to be very late. Anton and Liza were in danger!

We both started to get up. "We have to go," I

said. "Now!"

"You're not going anywhere until you're both patched up," said Vika.

"No, you don't understand. We have to get back. If he thinks we've run away he'll…" I caught myself just in time.

"You mean Evanko? What?" asked Mike. "He'll what?"

"Please, we can't say. We just have to get back."

Mike looked at me for a second, then at Dmitry. "How about you patch that one and I'll patch this one. Then we can drive them back.

CHAPTER 16

The Troops

Vika and Mike dressed our wounds as well as they could. They iced my ankle and wrapped it with an elastic bandage. I could already walk better, but they insisted I use the crutches that Mike had found in the storeroom. Vika said I should get stitches above my eye, but overall, I didn't feel that bad.

Dmitry's hand was severely hurt. It had been stepped on more than once while we were trying to crawl our way out of the "peaceful protest." Mike wrapped it up but said he'd probably need surgery. There was no way we could get to the hospital. The rioting was still going on. We could hear people yelling and screaming and the occasional gunshot. Vika said He wouldn't let us get anywhere near that free-for-all.

Before we left for the school, Vika made an announcement to his employees over the PA system in the warehouse.

"Could I please, have your attention everyone. This is Vika speaking. As you know, the protests have become violent. Travel in many areas of town isn't safe. For those of you who feel that you can't

F. B. VENEZIANO

make it home safely, we'll be keeping the warehouse open. You're all free to spend the night. We'll check the armory to see if we can secure some cots, and of course, linens are plentiful. We'll also make a food run. Julia will be making a list of who'll be staying so we'll know how much food to bring back. She'll also make arrangements for anyone who needs to make a call.

"We only have about an hour and a half of daylight left, so if you plan to leave, go now, and please, be careful."

Vika switched off the PA and turned to Mike.

"Mike, bring the truck around, we need to hustle."

Then he asked Julia. "Did you get all that?" she nodded.

"I want you to stay here, with me tonight, OK?"

It was clear that they were more than receptionist and boss. He touched her gently on the arm as he spoke. She mumbled, "Be careful," then grabbed a notepad and pencil, and left to take the count.

"Let's get out of here," Vika said. We saw Mike pull up, and rushed out.

"Hop in the back, boys," said Mike.

The truck was really a commercial van. The back, where Dmitry and I were riding, was fitted on one side with shelving, sized to accommodate wrapped linens for delivery. On the opposite side, were large baskets for sacks of dirty linens. We pulled out a couple of bags and sat on them.

Mike took a more southern route back to the school to avoid the protest. The walk to the warehouse had taken us more than an hour and a half. The return ride, just a few minutes.

One of the gates was always kept open during the day, for all deliveries including mail. No one had closed it yet, so we drove right through and stopped at the front door. When Mr. Evanko saw the truck pull up, he came outside, straightaway.

"Mr. Burick, an unexpected pleasure. What brings you here? Have these imps done something? Because if they have, I promise you, they'll be dealt with by me, personally."

"Dealt with, how?" Mike snapped.

"And, you are? Mr. Evanko asked coldly.

"My general manager and best friend," Vika said hurriedly. "You haven't heard about the riots, have you?"

Mr. Evanko backed off immediately.

"Riots? No. My wife called earlier to say there were protests in front of the courthouse, but she said nothing about riots."

"Perhaps we could talk inside. This January weather is freezing," said Mike. He rubbed his hands together.

Mr. Evanko looked over at Vika, who raised his eyebrows, questioningly, as if to say, *Well, can we?*

"Yes, of course. Come, right this way." He motioned toward the front door. "You two, report to your dorm supervisor."

"Hold on, boys," said Mike.

"They stay." Vika offered no further explanation. He turned and walked inside. We followed.

Mike began by explaining about the pickup at the hospital and how Dmitry and I had been caught in the middle of the unrest.

"You haven't questioned the boys' injuries," Vika said to Mr. Evanko.

"I saw them, of course. I just assumed the two of them had gotten into some more trouble."

Mike and Vika glared at him but didn't comment.

"And now you know—there's no fault here. Alex will need stitches and an X-ray of his ankle. Dmitry has several broken bones in his hand and may require surgery. He was in a lot of pain, so I called my private physician, Dr. Holda. He approved some medication that I was given for a broken wrist a couple of months ago.

"Dmitry took one before we drove them here, and he's to take the other one at bedtime. He has it. Is that a problem, or should I give it to someone in charge?" Vika paused, waiting for a response.

"Only one pill, you say?" asked Mr. Evanko.

"Yes, just one," answered Vika.

"Well, if it's just one pill, I suppose I can trust him to take it at the appropriate time."

"These boys were hurt doing me a service," Vika continued, "and I feel responsible. Therefore, I'll be picking both of them up, first thing in the morning, to take them to Dr. Holda for treatment. Their well-being is of *great importance* to me."

"That's not necessary," said Mr. Evanko.

"I insist." Vika stood and turned his back,

indicating that he was finished with the conversation. It was almost funny to see someone do to Andrey Evanko what he does to everyone else.

"We'll see you in the morning, boys."

As Mr. Evanko left to walk them out to their car, Dmitry and I took the opportunity to make a break for it!

First, we went to the dorm but realized it was supper time. We hadn't eaten since breakfast, and we were starving!

News of the riots had reached the school. The television in the common room was surrounded two deep, with kids and adults watching the evening broadcast. Still, Anton managed to spot me the minute I entered the room. He ran over and threw his arms around me. He was crying. I leaned the crutches against the wall and held him.

"I thought you were dead! You didn't come back, and then we heard about the riots. Two people died! Thirty more were hurt. They're in the hospital. I was so scared!"

"Dmitry!" It was Liza. She was running straight for him. Misha and Natalia were right behind her. He raised his broken hand above his head to protect it. Liza stopped short.

"Your hand!" she yelled.

"It'll be OK, Liza. I'm seeing the doctor in the morning," Dmitry told her.

"Man, am I glad to see you two. We thought you had bit the bullet!" said Misha.

"Misha! What an awful thing to say to them," yelled Natalia.

"How would you say it? They were getting shot at."

Janko stood up in the middle of the crowded common room and screamed at us.

"Shut up over there. We're trying to hear this!"

President Ebuchowski was speaking. We stepped in close enough to hear. He was talking about the riots downtown. He explained that it was an unprovoked attack on the police of Pervaiske. He said the protesters were heavily armed.

"That's not true!" said Dmitry.

"Shhh!"

"Today, at two fifteen, the Parliament of Ekrunia passed Anti-Protest legislation, which I have signed into law. The new law will accomplish, among other things, the following:

"Extremist activity has been criminalized. Violators will be fined and imprisoned.

"The penalty for blocking government buildings is up to five years in jail. The penalty for blocking an entrance to a residence is up to three years, for restriction of liberty. The unauthorized installation of tents, stages and sound equipment will result in fifteen days in jail. Participating in peaceful gatherings while wearing a mask, camouflage clothing, scarf, helmet, or other means of concealing or protecting one's face or head will be illegal and will also be punishable by up to fifteen days in jail.

"Beginning immediately, trials in absentia, including sentencing prison terms, are allowed for any violator who fails to appear in court for criminal proceedings.

"Amnesty from prosecution is applied to all military, police, and security forces for crimes committed against illegal protesters. Although, it's my opinion that stopping illegal protestors and others breaking our laws is hardly a crime.

"However, in keeping with the letter of the law, amnesty is officially declared."

Not a sound was heard in the room. Everyone was in shock. Then came the clincher.

"And lastly, I have decided to declare martial law both in the capital city of Kharvisk and the entire oblast of Luhansk, including Pervaiske."

Mrs. Galey let out a gasp. "*No*! Not again."

"One thousand troops have been assigned in the capital. Five hundred soldiers are being dispatched to Pervaiske. Police and security troops will enforce the law in other regions of Luhansk, and another two thousand troops are on standby for deployment in and around the Donetsk area, should the protests spread.

"This evening, curfews will take effect between the hours of nine p.m. and six a.m. Anyone on the streets during these hours will be subject to arrest.

"In conclusion, let me say this; we have come a very long way from the days before the revolution. Any form of insurgency against the government is an attack against its people. We must unite against those who would destroy the peace we have acquired through the blood of all those who came before us. I urge all citizens of Ekrunia to stand behind and work with your government to stop these dissenters in their tracks. Good night."

Mrs. Galey stood up and turned off the television.

"All right," she said, "everyone, back to the dining room. Get your supper and sit down."

Everyone spoke in a whisper while having supper.

"What does all that mean?" asked Anna.

"I'm not sure, but I think the soldiers are coming here to keep people off the streets," said Liza.

"It sounded like more than that to me," said Dmitry.

"What did it mean when the president said the police and soldiers who commit crimes against the protesters would get amnesty? What's amnesty?" asked Anton.

"It means that the police who killed those two people today won't have to answer for it. They can do whatever they want to people and get away with it," I answered.

"That's not fair!" said Anna.

"Misha, you're very quiet. What do you think?" asked Natalia.

"I think I'm glad that I'm not the one delivering laundry into town!" He laughed.

"You're not going to keep delivering the laundry to the warehouse, are you?" a wide-eyed Anton asked.

"If Mr. Evanko says to deliver the laundry, we deliver the laundry," said Dmitry.

"Alex, he can't make you go after those people got shot, can he?" Anton persisted.

"Sure, he can," said Misha.

"Listen," I told Anton, "the soldiers will keep things quiet during the day, and if there's trouble with the curfew, well, I'll be back by then. Besides, the warehouse is a mile away from the courthouse. We don't go anywhere near it."

"Really? Then how did you get hurt at the courthouse?" he asked sarcastically.

"That was a one-time thing, a fluke. We'll never have to go back there. So, you see, there's nothing to worry about."

I'm not sure he was convinced.

***

After supper, the adults turned the television

back on and were listening to the same information they had heard earlier, just said by a different face.

We had heard enough, so when Liza and Natalia said they were going to their dorm, Dmitry and I played cards with Anna and Anton, in a far corner of the room. After a couple of games, everyone seemed to lose interest.

"Why don't we all go to bed early?" I suggested. "It's been a long day."

We went up to the second floor. I watched Anton as he walked Anna to her dorm. He turned and walked a few feet, then went into his dorm.

At that moment, I felt so much love for my little brother. I reaffirmed my promise to myself that I would never turn my back on him the way Irina and Papa did. I would never walk out on him, not ever.

***

I was sleeping, when the sounds of a loud commotion in the halls woke me. I sat up and tried to focus in the darkness. Someone close to the door switched on the light. The door opened. Boys and girls alike were rushing down the hall. I got out of bed, reached for the crutches, but decided to leave them. I hobbled along until I spotted Dmitry, who was in the hall talking to Liza.

"What's going on?" I asked.

Just then, one of the older boys from the upper secondary dorm yelled from the landing, "Tanks!"

We looked at each other and ran towards the landing. Well, they ran, I hobbled. There were kids everywhere. We couldn't get to either dorm with windows, so we went upstairs to the third floor.

When we got to the front windows, a few kids were already there. We looked out and saw a long caravan of cargo trucks led by several jeeps and followed by three tanks. The back of each truck was full of soldiers dressed in full battle gear. The convoy was so loud that I couldn't believe the noise didn't penetrate our windowless inner chambers.

"Why would they be coming this way? Downtown is west of us. Wouldn't they go southeast to get there from Kharvisk?" Dmitry asked.

"Not if they're coming from the army base in Lychansk," I answered. "I'm going to find Anton."

I was afraid the sight of this "invasion" might make him nervous.

When I got to his dorm, he was looking out the window with the other kids.

"Hey," I said.

"Alex! Did you see? Tanks and soldiers. There's so many. It's like a parade."

He didn't sound frightened at all, more like excited. The military caravan was quite a sight.

Right about then, all the dorm supervisors started rounding up everyone from both the third and second floors. Everyone was sent back where they belonged with a stern warning to stay there.

After lights-out for the second time that night, Dmitry slipped over to my bed, and we sat up and talked for a while.

"So, what do you think? Are we delivering laundry to town the rest of the week?"

"Not tomorrow," I said. "Tomorrow we go to the doctor."

"Oh right. Those pills worked so well, I almost forgot." He looked at his hand. "Well, we'd better get some sleep. Nite, Alex."

"Nite, Dmitry."

CHAPTER 17

The Surprise

The summer came and went. It was September. The troops remained in Pervaiske, enforcing the curfew and the ban on protests. The strikes continued, but the soldiers immediately squelched any sign of an assembly or demonstration. The strikers who tried to march were arrested The jail was overcrowded with so-called dissidents, and when they ran out of room there, the armory was converted to hold more.

By autumn, people were getting more and more willful and aggressive. With winter coming, no income, and no sign of the impasse coming to any conclusion, intrepid crowds were gathering in the square more often and with increasing numbers. It was clear that the government was waiting them out, confident that when their families started freezing and starving, the people would be more agreeable to the miserable pittance the government was willing to pay them, something is better than nothing. Tensions were growing.

Things at the boarding school went on as usual. The school garden had produced a substantial bounty. What wasn't stolen or sold should have been enough to feed all of us, but it didn't seem to be.

The garden wasn't the only thing that had grown over the summer. Dmitry and I had shot up nearly three inches each, and with the help of Mike's sandwiches and Cokes, had bulked up proportionately. The others had also grown. Anton was almost the size I was when all this had started, eons ago. Misha was a year younger than Dmitry, but only about an inch shorter.

Natalia and Liza were growing into womanhood. They had developed curves in all the right places. This didn't go unnoticed by Janko, and the girls said it was getting harder to keep him at arms' length.

Dmitry's hand had healed well, thanks to Dr. Holda's expert care.

We were still delivering to the warehouse every day, and Mike always had sandwiches and Cokes waiting for us. He and Vika had become an essential part of our lives. After their visit with Mr. Evanko, living at the orphanage seemed a little easier. Even Janko backed off a bit. We found ourselves spending more, and more time at the laundry, helping Mike and Vika by running errands.

Dmitry had been permanently transferred to the

school laundry. Mr. Chorney pitched a fit the first time we were late coming back, but when Vika found out, he made a simple call to Mr. Evanko, and we were never questioned by our boss again. Mr. Chorney never said anything, but we could sense his anger and loathing.

***

It was a beautiful, crisp, fall day. Dmitry and I were taking our usual route to the warehouse. The leaves were beginning to turn, and the colors were beautiful.

"Let's break for a minute," said Dmitry. "It's so nice here."

We were early, so there couldn't be any harm in stopping.

We lay down in the tall weeds beside a small knoll. The fall wildflowers were sprinkled through the field in brilliant colors.

"When do you think the army will leave?" asked Dmitry.

"I don't know. If the workers don't stop the strike, they could be here for a long time." I answered.

"Seems to me that things can't go on like this

forever. Something's got to give. How will people make it through the winter?" asked Dmitry.

"A lot of them might not make it!" I answered.

We didn't talk much after that. We just took in the day.

"Well, we'd better get going," I said after a while.

"Hold on," said Dmitry.

He got up and picked a bunch of wildflowers.

"For Julia," he said.

Julia, the secretary, turned out to be OK. Her condescending attitude that first day was never repeated. Instead, she smiled and spoke nicely every time we went near the front office. Most likely because of our friendship with Vika. It was clear that she would do anything to please him. But in Dmitry's mind, she was nice because it was just in her nature. He had developed quite an affection for her.

We arrived at the warehouse, went around to the employee entrance, and walked in.

"Surprise!!" yelled Mike, Vika and several employees, including Daria. They led us into the

lunchroom.

I had no idea what was going on. The room was decorated with balloons and streamers. Anton, Liza, Misha, Natalia, and even Anna were there. They ran forward yelling "Happy birthday!"

"What? How did you all get here? Why…"

Anton spoke first. "Mike picked us up. It's your birthday. Did you forget?"

"Hell, yeah, I forgot!"

"What about Mr. Evanko? Does he know you're all here?"

"Yes," said Liza, "Vika arranged it."

"And we don't have to be back at any special time," smiled Anna. "This is so exciting; we never get to go anywhere!"

"Did you know about this?" I asked Dmitry. He shrugged, still holding the flowers he had picked for Julia.

"It was his job to slow you down so we could get here first and set up," Misha said as Dmitry walked over and gave Julia the flowers. She smiled gratefully and touched his arm. He would float through the rest of the party.

"Vika, how did you get Mr. Evanko to go along with this?" I asked.

"He puts a lot of money in his pocket because of our little deal. He knows it would cost him, to be on my bad side."

"But you said that dealing with him wasn't up to you. It was "the powers that be," I said, making quotation marks with my index and middle fingers.

"Well, that was my father, and since he's chosen to retire and turn the business over to me, as of now, I am "the powers that be." He's lived in Poland for five years now. It's about time he turned the reins over to his only heir. Besides, too late to break the contract now. I like having you guys around. Just don't tell that to Evanko."

"OK," yelled Mike, "time for the cake."

As Mike lit the candles on my birthday cake, they all sang "Happy Birthday."

"Make a wish," said Anton.

"Not so fast," said Mike.

Julia came walking in with another cake.

"Since your birthdays are only two weeks apart, we decided to combine them," she said. "Anton, come on over. It's your turn."

He looked up at me in disbelief. This birthday was the first we had celebrated in years; Papa didn't like the fuss. And we were celebrating together.

This time, they sang "Happy Birthday" to Anton. We each made a wish. I looked around at the faces of the people I had come to love like family, and I wished I could freeze time.

Well, that's never going to happen. Make a real wish, I thought. So I wished we could all be together for my next birthday.

When Anton finished his wish, we blew out our candles. We were, clearly, a bit emotional after sharing such an incredible moment.

"Let's eat!" someone shouted.

As Julia was cutting the cakes and serving one piece from each to everyone, Mike came over and whispered something in Vika's ear.

"Save me a piece. I'll be back in a few minutes,"

Vika got up and went into his office. Just before he closed the door, I noticed some men inside.

We sat eating the delicious cake while the employees came over one or two at a time, to wish us happy birthday and to thank us jokingly for their afternoon off work.

When Vika finished his meeting, he joined us for cake. I stood with my Coke held high and toasted Mike and Vika.

"To the two men who have made such a difference in our lives. Thank you for taking the time to care."

"It's not my birthday, kid, knock it off before I cry!" Mike teased.

Everyone laughed and took a drink.

After the party, we got a ride back to the school from Mike. Another cool memory

CHAPTER 18

The Call

"Hey, smartass! Get to Mr. Evanko's office, pronto," Janko hollered as sweet as ever.

"Me? Why? What's up?" I asked.

"Just get your ass down there before I make you wish you hadn't asked me questions!"

Time was, he would have acted on that threat. I was becoming more and more convinced, that Mr. Evanko had said something to protect his business arrangement. Did that explain Janko's restraint?

I rushed down to the office. Mr. Evanko was talking on the phone. He was smiling and being very pleasant to the person on the other end of the line.

I turned to wait in the outer office until he had finished, but he called me back.

"Well, here he is now. Hold on, and I'll pass him the phone."

His smile faded as he reached out with the phone in his hand. He looked enraged but controlled his emotions well. His face was red, and his hand shook as I took the phone from him.

"Hello?"

"Hey, kid, it's me, Mike. Vika asked me to give you a call."

"Hi, Mike, what's up?" I tried to sound nonchalant, you know like having Mr. Evanko take my calls was an everyday occurrence. Inside, my stomach was in my throat, and my heart wasn't far behind.

"You need to be careful coming to the warehouse today. Something might be going on in the square. Don't discuss it with Evanko. If he asks questions, which I'm sure he will tell him I'm calling about a pickup I need you to get on your way in."

I glanced over. Mr. Evanko was pacing impatiently, and staring in my direction.

"Just come straight here and stay away from the square, OK?"

"OK, Mike, sure. I'll see you later."

I handed the phone back to Mr. Evanko and thanked him. He sat at his desk and hung up.

"I'm not your personal secretary," he said.

"What's so important that I have to take calls for you in my office?"

"Mike needs us to make a pickup on the way to the warehouse," I answered. "Thank you, again, sir. Have a nice day."

I was gone before he could respond. If he pushed me for details, I'd be hard-pressed to come up with answers.

I found Dmitry eating breakfast with the others. I grabbed a tray and filled it up with bread and juice. By the time I got to the table, all eyes were on me. They were anxious to know what was going on.

Anton spoke up first. "Why did you have to go to Mr. Evanko's office? Are you in trouble?"

"You're not going to believe this," I said somewhat seriously.

It worked. They were dreading what was, they were sure, to be horrible news. Dmitry and Liza looked at each other and then back to me, waiting.

"What?!" Anton had grown impatient.

"I had a call."

Everyone sat silently, waiting for the punch line.

"I had a phone call...from Mike," I answered

looking down at my hands.

"What happened? Is Vika all right?" Dmitry looked so frightened that I decided the joke had gone far enough.

"He's OK. Everything's fine. I was just kidding." I started laughing.

"That's not even a little bit funny. Don't ever pull a stunt like that again!" Dmitry punched me in the arm.

"So why did Mike call?" asked Anton, still chuckling.

"Oh yeah, what did Mike want?" asked Dmitry.

"He wanted to warn us to be careful going over there today. Something might be going on in the square."

"How does he know something might be going on?" Dmitry asked.

"What's going on in the square?" asked Misha.

"He didn't say. He just told me to be careful and don't talk to Mr. Evanko about it."

"A phone call in Mr. Evanko's office?" asked Anna.

"Yup."

"On *his* phone," said Liza.

"Yup."

"And Mr. Evanko had to take the call…for you? Like a secretary?" asked Anton.

I gave them my biggest smile.

Their laughter filled the dining room.

"Can you imagine Mr. Evanko?" said Natalia. "Call for you, Mr. Krisko. Would you like to take it in my office, Mr. Krisko? Here, take my seat, Mr. Krisko. Do make yourself at home!"

Her imitation of him had us in stitches. We were laughing so loud that Mrs. Galey had to come over and tell us to quiet down.

"Well, we'd better get to school," said Dmitry.

***

After class, we picked up the clean linens and left to go to the warehouse.

We didn't talk much on the walk over. When we got there, everything was normal. We brought the clean laundry over to Daria. After she had signed off on the delivery, I started to go to Vika's office to ask him about the call, but he was in another meeting. So I headed to the lunchroom.

When I got there, Mike and Dmitry were talking. I walked over and sat down.

"Hi. I was telling Dmitry that rumor has it, the protests might start up again. Things are getting pretty edgy. It seems the people are tired of waiting for the government to make a move."

"Seems to me they already made a move when they sent soldiers to enforce martial law," I replied.

"A lot of people feel the same way," Mike said. "When the protests start, it won't take long before riots break out. It's going to be a lot worse than it was the day you boys got caught in the middle."

"Anything you need us to do down there before it starts?" asked Dmitry.

"Nope. Just get your pickup and head back to the school while it's still quiet. And boys, let's keep this between us. No sense making everyone nervous."

We went out back counted the pieces for pickup and signed them out. As we left, several men were also leaving by the back. They must have been the men in the meeting. They smiled and waved at Vika, who had walked them out.

When Vika saw us, he walked over and asked, "Did Mike talk to you guys?"

"Hi, Vika. Yeah, he did."

"Good. Let's hold off on any deliveries for a couple of days. I'll call Evanko. He'll tell you when to make the next delivery. Now, get back and keep your heads up, OK?"

We nodded as Vika went back inside.

On the return trip, we talked about this trouble Vika and Mike were so sure was about to happen.

"What do you think?" asked Dmitry.

"I don't know. It's all kinda weird. Mike and Vika seem pretty sure trouble is coming," I said.

"How do they know?"

"They must hear a lot more than we do out at the school," I said.

"A lot of people are gonna get hurt," said Dmitry.

We agreed not to mention it to anyone when we got back.

***

"To what do we owe the pleasure of your company so early in the day?" Mr. Chorney snapped as we walked into the laundry.

"Just slummin'," laughed Dmitry.

Mr. Chorney grabbed him by the front of his shirt, got in his face, and spoke in a low, controlled voice.

"You think you're hot shit because the boss says you're off limits for now, but let me tell you something. Boss or no boss, you get mouthy with me again, and I'll make sure your mouth won't work for a while."

He shoved Dmitry back, slowly walked into his office, and closed the door.

Well, I guessed my theory was right. We *were* off limits.

Liza came over and punched Dmitry in the arm.

"Ow!" he said

Through gritted teeth, in what could be called a loud whisper, Liza said, "What's the matter with you, pushing him like that? Do you want to get beaten?"

"Come on; I was just joking. I can't help it if

Chorney has no sense of humor."

Liza gave Dmitry a look that stopped him in his tracks. He got quiet and looked down at his feet.

"I'm sorry, Liza." he murmured and started unloading and sorting the linens from the warehouse.

Time flew by. No one spoke. We just did our jobs. We finished our work and left to go to supper.

The menu consisted of cabbage soup, bread, and potato pancakes. We got our food and sat down.

"Why *were* you back so early today?" asked Liza.

"We finished up early. That's all," I said.

My answer seemed to satisfy her.

"See? It's all good," smiled Dmitry.

We finished eating and cleaned up our trays. We walked over to the TV. Dmitry and I were anxious to see if anything had happened. When we turned it on, the pictures behind the newscaster shocked us. It was utter chaos! Gunfire, people were screaming, and throwing things at soldiers who were shooting tear gas into the crowd.

"They were right," whispered Dmitry. "How *did*

they know.

CHAPTER 19

The Oversight

Dmitry and I knew we weren't supposed to make any deliveries to the warehouse; Vika had been clear on that. So after school, we reported to work in the laundry.

We were worried about Mike and Vika, and we tried to think of a way we could get to the warehouse anyway.

"I say we just walk out when no one's looking," said Dmitry.

"And what happens to Liza and Anton when Mr. Evanko finds out? Did you forget what he said about them paying for what we do?" I asked.

When we walked into the laundry, Mr. Chorney was in his office. We began packing the linen delivery in a basket to set aside until we had permission to go back to the warehouse.

Mr. Chorney came out of his office and began shouting at us.

"You two wanna hurry and get that shit out of here? It's holding up the folding table, and we're behind schedule!"

"You! Get that laundry in the washing machines. You, Empty those dryers!" He walked around the room giving orders.

We looked at each other in disbelief. Could it be that Mr. Chorney hadn't gotten the word?

"Do you think he doesn't know?" I asked Dmitry. He shrugged and smiled.

"You heard the man," said Dmitry. "Let's get this shit outa here."

I couldn't believe our luck.

***

We were about halfway to town when we noticed the smell of burning wood. As we got closer, the scent became stronger, and we could see smoke above the trees. When we got to the edge of town on Kuibyshanka Street, our way was blocked by three armed soldiers standing in front of a makeshift blockade of fifty-gallon drums and sawhorses. One of the soldiers was accompanied by a big dog that sat vigilantly at his side.

"What do you think we should do?" I slowed my pace as we got closer to the checkpoint.

"Too late. Just keep smiling like you've just seen your best friend," answered Dmitry.

With confidence in his walk, a wave, and a smile, he made it look easy. I tried to follow his lead by putting on a confident air of my own, but I knew I was just whistling in the dark. I hoped the soldiers didn't.

We approached them cautiously. The dog stood to attention and looked at us appraisingly. He made a quiet, menacing growl.

"*Sydity*," the dog's handler yelled. The dog sat, but his stare never wavered.

"Where do you two think you're going?" snapped the soldier.

"To the laundry warehouse, sir," I answered, still trying to compose my nerves.

"What is your business there, and where are you coming from?"

"We're delivering clean linens to Burick's Linen Rental. The warehouse is just down the street. We wash them in the laundry at Pervaiske Boarding School," said Dmitry with a big smile on his face.

"It's a few miles in that direction." I pointed east. "You passed it on your way into the city when your convoy arrived."

"So you're orphans?" It was more of a statement than a question. "Let's have a look. Put the basket on the ground."

As we complied, the dog and his handler came closer. We stepped away from the basket to what I foolishly considered a safe distance. Then it occurred to me, if that leash comes off, we can't get far enough to be safe.

They walked around the basket while the dog sniffed.

"I need to see. Dump it on the ground," instructed the guard. He looked amused.

"But the linens will get dirty," I weakly protested.

He kicked the basket over, spilling its contents all over the ground. Dmitry began to take a step forward, and the soldier pointed his weapon directly at him. Dmitry froze. I nearly jumped out of my skin. The dog began digging through the laundry and sniffing. He left dirt and paw prints all over the now unfolded heap.

"Looks OK. What do you think, comrades?" he yelled over his shoulder to his friends. They all began laughing.

"Pick it up. You're free to go," he said, but his weapon still pointed in our direction. We were both frozen to the spot.

"Now!"

Finally, he lowered his gun, and we walked cautiously toward the basket. We put the linens back in the basket and hurried on our way.

"What a bunch of funny guys, huh?" Dmitry said.

"I thought we were goners, for sure," I responded.

***

There were fire trucks in the street in front of the warehouse. We tried to get to it, but the police were keeping the crowd at bay. We watched helplessly from across the street, trying to get a glimpse of Mike or Vika.

Without warning, someone grabbed Dmitry and me by the arm, pulling us to the side.

"What the hell are you doing here? You were both told to stay put until you heard from us!"

It was Mike. His face was red, and the vein in his neck was pulsing.

"We saw on television what was happening. We just wanted to be sure everyone was all right," stammered Dmitry.

"We want to help," I said.

"Help? What, you can put out major fires now? Come with me."

Mike took us over to the truck which was parked just down the street from the warehouse.

"Get in."

"But, the basket," I protested.

"Leave it!"

We got into the back. Vika turned around from the front seat and saw us just as Mike got behind the wheel and started the truck.

"What the hell are you doing here?" said Vika.

"That's what I said," Mike replied. "We've got to get them out of here. It's not safe."

"There's a roadblock back the way we came," I said.

"There are roadblocks on every road coming into the city. How did you get through?" asked Mike.

"We turned on our boyish charm," smiled Dmitry. Mike wasn't amused.

"This isn't a joke, kid. People are getting killed!" Mike slammed his fist on the steering wheel.

"Did they give you a hard time?" asked Vika.

I looked at Mike then at Vika. "Yes, one of them pulled a gun on us."

"Let's go to my apartment," Vika told Mike.

"You'll have to stay with me for a couple of days," he said to us.

"No, we can't," I said. "When Mr. Evanko finds out we came without permission; he'll punish Anton and Liza!"

"You should have thought of that before you put yourselves in this situation!" shouted Mike.

I was stunned into silence. I looked over to Dmitry. He looked as if the blood had been drained from his body. We should have thought it through. Now, because of our impulsiveness, Vika and Mike were infuriated with us, and worse, Anton and Liza were going to face the consequences.

"Easy, Mike." Vika placed a hand on his arm.

"I'll take care of it, boys. I'll call Mr. Evanko when we get to the apartment."

***

Vika's apartment was on the second floor of a brick building a couple of miles from the warehouse. The front door opened directly into a large living room. On the wall straight ahead was a big window that overlooked the city. Against another wall was a white leather sectional that popped against the tan-colored walls. The room was trimmed in white. Through an arched doorway next to the sectional was the kitchen, modern and bright. To the left were two bedrooms.

Vika walked over to the side table and dialed the phone.

"Andrey? Vika here. Listen, I have Alex and Dmitry at my place…No, no, we got our wires crossed, the boys didn't know. I thought Mike had told them, and he thought I had…I know it is, and I apologize…Well, that won't be easy, Andrey. Leaving right now is tough. Roadblocks surround the city. They're searching for the insurgents that started the fires. I'm afraid I'll have to keep the boys here for a couple of days until things settle down a little…No, no more than a couple of days I should think, I'll keep you posted. OK? *Do pobačennja* (Good-bye)."

Vika hung up the phone and turned to us. "Mike and I have to check on the warehouse. Don't leave the apartment, and don't answer the door. If it's us, we won't be knocking."

Vika rounded up some clean clothes for us.

"Take a shower and get something to eat from the kitchen. Make yourselves at home. We'll probably be late. You two can take the small bedroom there."

After they left, we walked around to get familiar with our temporary lodgings. There was so much food in the refrigerator that we had a hard time deciding what to eat. We weren't used to so many good choices. We finally settled on ham sandwiches and a couple of sodas. We ate and showered, then sat down on the couch and turned on the television. It was dark outside, so we turned on a light.

The news was about the situation in Pervaiske. They were showing live transmissions and comparing them to the video from the night before.

Out in the distance, we heard popping sounds. We went to the window to look out. It was past curfew, but we could see some men running down the street. We quickly turned out the light so we wouldn't be seen, and watched.

Soldiers were shooting at them. Another man was kneeling under a streetlight, and one of the soldiers was holding a gun to his head. When the group of men was gone from sight, the soldier tied the man's hands behind his back. Another put him in the back of a car and took him away.

By midnight, Mike and Vika hadn't returned. We figured they had gotten stuck in the warehouse because of the curfew. We went to bed, but I couldn't sleep. I was a bundle of nerves. I just lay there listening to sporadic gunshots in the distance, wondering if Anton was all right back at the school. I glanced over at Dmitry. His eyes were closed, but I could tell by his rapid breathing, that his mind was in the same place. Eventually, sleep came.

***

When we woke up the next morning, Vika and Mike were in the kitchen.

"What time did you get back? I never heard you come in." I was surprised to see them.

"It was late. Did you find everything you needed?" asked Vika.

"Yeah, sure. How bad is the warehouse?"

"Not too bad," said Mike. "The fire was confined to the front. It looks like an RCID went astray and through the office window."

"A what?" Dmitry and I both asked.

"RCID. It means riot control incendiary device. They started using them in the Middle East a few years ago. It's like shooting a fireball. The device is ignited at the point of ejection and bingo! You aim, shoot, and people either run or catch fire, sometimes both!" said Mike.

"In this case, they missed their target and nearly burned down my building," added Vika.

"We saw some guy get arrested last night," I said.

Mike snapped, "I told you not to leave–"

"We didn't! We saw it through the window," I told him. "Some other guys managed to get away, even though the soldiers were shooting at them."

"There was a lot of shooting last night," said Dmitry.

"Do you think Anton could hear the shots at the school?" I asked Mike.

"It was a clear night, could be," he answered.

"He's probably scared, and I'm worried about him. When can we go back?" I asked.

"They aren't letting vehicles in or out of the city. When you do go back, you'll have to walk your usual route. Soldiers are patrolling all the surrounding neighborhoods. If they catch you trying to sneak out of the city that way, they'll shoot first and ask questions later. So that leaves the roadblock you passed on the road into town. The guards are probably jumpy as hell.

"Let's give it another day or two. If things aren't any quieter by then, we'll figure out a way to get you back, OK?" Vika told us.

"You boys play cards?"

"Sure, I play a mean game of drunkard," Dmitry said.

They looked at each other and laughed.

"Come over and sit down. Mike and I are going to teach you a real man's game. Ever heard of poker?

CHAPTER 20

No Negotiating

We were at Vika's for the second day. He and Mike were teaching Dmitry and me to play poker. Note I said they were teaching us, not that we were learning. As a result, I lost about two hundred matches before we played for candy. I lost all my candy, and then we played for work time. I lost.

Long story short, I owed Vika twelve hundred minutes of free labor. Of course, my labor had always been free, so I guess the joke was on him. Dmitry was worse off. He owed over seventeen hundred minutes, three days!

We split the extra day and were going to work two-and-a-half days each rebuilding the damaged office at the warehouse. We would have done it anyway, but it was more fun this way.

Mike and Vika left after the poker game the night before to stay in the warehouse and protect it from looters. When Dmitry and I got up the next morning, they were already back.

"How were things at the warehouse last night?" I asked.

"It was quiet. No break-in's with top-notch guards like us on duty," said Mike.

"Truth be told, I was the only top-notch guard on duty, but I didn't have to work very hard. Mike's snoring scared off all the looters on our side of town," laughed Vika.

"We heard a lot of gunfire around three o'clock. What happened?" asked Dmitry.

"Snipers, shooting at the soldiers. The gunfire seemed to be coming from the abandoned apartment buildings behind the courthouse. But if anyone was there they split before the soldiers arrived," answered Mike.

"You two about ready to remodel an office?" asked Vika.

"Let's go," I responded.

People were filling the streets, milling around on corners and in front of shops. Military vehicles patrolled the streets while soldiers made futile attempts to break up crowds. Those who weren't arrested ran and gathered somewhere else.

We were stopped twice by soldiers checking identification, asking where we were going and why. Vika told them about the warehouse and explained that Dmitry and I were from the orphanage and would be working on the repairs.

As we got closer to the center of town, we saw protesters congregated in the square. They were taunting the soldiers who were guarding the courthouse where the military had set up its headquarters. The protesters were carrying signs that said things like, "Negotiate Now" and "Just Wages for Honest Work." They were shouting in unison, "Bohdan Ebuchowski, bargain fairly!"

About a block from the square, we were stopped again and detained by the military. We were questioned and told to step out of the truck. As they checked Vika and Mike's identification, the officer in charge ordered the other two to search the vehicle.

"What are you looking for?" Mike asked.

The officer must have thought a bit too belligerently. Mike stepped in front of the soldier, who took it to as a sign of aggression. He pushed Mike back against the truck with his rifle, stepped back and aimed it directly at Mike's head.

Vika quickly stepped in front of Mike with his hands up in front of him.

"Easy. My friend didn't mean anything, did you, buddy?" Vika looked at Mike then back to the officer in charge. Vika smiled broadly.

"We're happy to cooperate with you. Search away. There's nothing in there to hide. Please."

Vika guardedly moved aside still in front of Mike. He guided Mike back by placing his left arm on Mike's chest.

Dmitry and I were standing a few feet in front of the truck during the entire altercation. We didn't dare move of course, but I felt surprisingly calm as I watched the drama unfolding in front of me. It was as if nothing terrible would happen as long as we were with Vika and Mike.

While the truck was being searched, the officer turned to us and demanded our identification, which of course we didn't have. Vika explained again about the warehouse damage and how we were from the orphanage and were working for him.

I saw Vika reach into his pocket and pull out some cash, which he offered to the officer. After a moment's hesitation, the officer looked around and took the money.

"Get proper identification for your workers, or next time they'll be arrested, understood?"

"You bet," smiled Vika. "And if you ever need the services of a good laundry, just stop by…on the house, of course. My people do excellent work."

He held out his hand. "Vika Burick."

The officer hesitated a minute then smiled. He put out his hand in response, and said, "*Molodshyl Leitenant* Benko."

"Junior Lieutenant Benko, it's a pleasure," said Vika.

Just then—gunfire! The protesters in the square were getting more forceful. They were demanding that someone in authority from Kharvisk open negotiations with their leaders. They had grown frustrated with being ignored and were throwing things at the soldiers.

Junior Lieutenant Benko called for his men to follow as he headed toward the disturbance. Just a few feet later, one of them fell. Vika and Mike yelled, "Get down!"

We hit the dirt without question. It was sniper fire. The junior lieutenant and his men dove behind the truck. They opened fire in the direction of the shooters, but it was useless. The snipers were too well hidden.

Convoy trucks pulled up to the square. Soldiers with batons, shields, rifles, and handguns got off and immediately attacked the crowd. Within seconds, the protesters were joined by more protesters who seemed to appear from nowhere. They were armed with axes, knives, truncheons, and corrugated iron shields. What followed was mayhem.

The snipers stopped shooting. Maybe they had been found by government forces, or perhaps they couldn't safely target soldiers without putting protesters in jeopardy. Whatever the reason, we took the opportunity to get into the truck. The junior lieutenant also realized the shooting had stopped and rushed with his men to the square.

Mike was behind the wheel. He put the truck into reverse, sped a few blocks and turned the wheel. As soon as the front of the truck started sliding, Mike pressed the brakes lightly and put the car in neutral. Half-way through the slide, he put the car in gear. As soon as the front was pointed in the right direction, he hit the accelerator. He finished the one-eighty, and took off away from the riots.

Dmitry and I were in the back, hanging on for dear life. My heart was thumping, my ears were ringing, and I could barely hear the gunshots or the screaming in the distance. My nostrils were filled with the smell of burning rubber.

When we arrived in front of the apartment building, Dmitry composed himself enough to say,

"Wow, can you teach me to drive, Mike?"

The laughter that followed eased the tension that filled the truck.

***

Once we were back in the apartment, Vika suggested that Dmitry and I make some lunch for everyone while he went into his bedroom to make a phone call. Mike went with him.

I made sandwiches, and Dmitry first defrosted and then warmed up some soup he found in the freezer.

We had nearly finished eating when there was a knock on the door. Vika got up to answer. It was one of the men I had seen in Vika's office a couple of times.

"This is Vlad Chaplinski, a friend of mine," Vika said to Dmitry and me.

"Vlad this is Alex and Dmitry. They're the kids from the boarding school that I told you about. Have a seat. We were just finishing lunch. Can I get you something?"

What did you tell him about us? I wondered.

"Just some coffee would be nice," said Vlad.

"I'll put some on," said Mike.

"I called Vlad for some help. You guys have to get back to the school. Things are getting very explosive, and it's not safe here," said Vika.

"It's not going to be easy. The military is spreading out its patrols," said Vlad. "I can get you out of town, but you'll be on your own from there."

He pulled out a piece of paper from his pocket. On it was a hand-drawn map of the terrain between the apartment and the school.

"Troops have been seen in these areas, here, here, and here." He drew X's on the areas with patrols.

"We'll get you to this point. From there stay in this section, and you should get back to the school with no problem. We'll leave in the morning before sunrise."

The Army of Orphans: The Beginning

Part II

"You're off to great places!
Today is your day!
Your mountain is waiting
So get on your way!"

Dr. Seuss

CHAPTER 21

The Cellar

We didn't sleep much that night; we just lay there on the bed with our clothes on, ready to leave. I was anxious to see Anton. He had never been on his own for so long.

Around four in the morning, there was a knock on the bedroom door, and then it opened.

"Ready?" Vika peeked around the door.

We walked into the kitchen where Mike, Vlad, and two other men were waiting.

"Danil, Eugene," said Vlad, "Alex and Dmitry." We nodded hello.

"We're going through the abandoned apartments behind the courthouse. Then we'll double back through the neighborhoods on Vyonoshka Street," said Vlad. "You get down when I signal, and you stay put until I signal you forward. Understand?"

We acknowledged with a nod.

"What about the snipers?" I asked.

Vlad looked over at Vika.

"Don't worry. We've got it covered," Vika answered.

"Let's go," said Vlad.

Mike and Vika gave us handshakes and hugs, wished us luck, and sent us on our way.

"If you need us, you know where we are," said Mike.

***

Here we go. Just like something out of a Spiderman comic. The good guys are quietly sneaking around the bad guys. Come on, stop shaking. Spidey wouldn't be scared. You have to get back to Anton. There's the signal, run.

OK, stop and stay put. Stop breathing so loud! Another signal, hurry, down the alley, behind the buildings. There, the apartment ruins, almost there.

We ran inside one of the buildings that had probably housed snipers the day before. Dmitry and I waited quietly for instructions while our three guides checked the area for soldiers.

Vlad gave the signal to move, and we followed him across a small field to the back of a house. We were in the Vyonoshka neighborhood. We followed the alleys southeast to more fields outside of town.

"This is as far as we go," said Vlad. "You got it from here?"

"Sure, we know exactly where we are," I responded.

"Remember to check the map for troops, and stay in the woods away from the railroad tracks; they're watching them. If you do get caught, don't run. Tell them you're from the orphanage and you thought it would be a good time to run away. You heard the guns, then changed your mind. You're just trying to get back."

"Will do, thanks," said Dmitry.

We took off and ran until we got to the old neighborhood ruins. We stopped behind one of the foundations to rest. In the distance, you could barely see where the trees met the sky. It was beginning to get light.

"We'd better hustle. The sun's coming up," I said.

We couldn't go on the tracks, so we found a safe place to cross to the east and headed north through the woods that ran beside the railroad tracks. We heard voices and ducked into an abandoned work shack. The sounds were no more than thirty feet away. They belonged to two guards who patrolled the tracks in opposite directions. When they met back in the middle, they stopped to share a cigarette.

We waited, barely breathing. I closed my eyes as tightly as I could. There were stars behind my lids. *Go away, don't come any closer, go away*, I kept saying over and over in my mind, willing them to go back to walking their stretches of track.

There was an explosion louder than any gunfire I had ever heard. The guards took off running in the direction of the blasts, and we jumped out the back window of the shack and hit the ground running!

When we were clear, we stopped to see what was going on. Against the early-morning sky, we saw some kind of projectiles heading straight toward town. Then we heard the sounds of destruction. From the direction of the explosion, we guessed it hit one of the abandoned apartment buildings.

More explosions, closer this time. We ran as fast as we could to the school. It wasn't hit, but the bombs were close enough to frighten everyone. When we got inside, the supervisors were yelling directions to screaming kids who could only hear the sound of fear. The supervisors were trying to get the kids into the cellar. There was an old shelter down there from another war, another time.

Liza saw us and came running over. She threw her arms around her brother, relieved to see him safely back.

"Where's Anton?" I yelled at her.

"I haven't seen him. We'll help you look!" Liza shouted back.

We ran up to the second floor. Mrs. Galey was directing her wards towards the stairs. I saw Anton just as he noticed me. We ran to each other and hugged. I pulled back to look at him. He had a black eye and a bloody cut on his swollen lip.

"Who did this to you?"

He just looked down. Anna answered for him.

"Mr. Janko."

I turned to Liza and Dmitry. "Hurry, grab what you can. We're getting the hell out of here!" I said above the chaos.

"Where are Natalia and Misha?"

"I'll find them," said Liza.

"Come right back!" I called after her.

Janko came down the hall pushing and yelling at kids. He saw me.

"What the hell are you doing back here? How did you get past the mortar bombs? You'd better get out of the way, smart ass, or I'll give you a little of what I gave this little piss ant."

He started to walk towards Anton; I stepped in front of him.

I felt anger rising; my face was hot, my fists clenched. Not your typical "I'm mad" anger, but a blind fury from deep within. Suddenly, it was as if my life flashed before me; Mama's death, Papa's abuse, Irina's betrayal, the fights, the beatings, Anton's pain. I began to shake. After years of fear and violence, I had reached my limit.

"No more!" I screamed, and like a madman, I flew at Janko with a rage that had been building for years.

My fists landed blow after blow with such lightning speed that Janko never got a chance defend himself. A group had gathered and watched in disbelief.

Finally, exhausted and spent, I fell back against the wall. My heart was pounding. Janko lay on the floor bleeding. Anton and Anna rushed to my side. I realized the sounds of the attack were still going on outside.

Dmitry ran up to me. He looked at Janko."What the hell?"

"Let's get out of here," I said. We left to find the others.

We found Liza with Natalia and Misha on the stairs and walked out unnoticed. We headed towards the ruins in the woods. We avoided the tracks by going north then cutting back.

At last, we arrived at the ruins. Dmitry found a cellar with an outside hatch hidden in the weeds. It was on the edge of the rubble and surrounded by trees. We opened the doors and went in. It was very dark inside, and it was hard to see. The only light was from the open door. It was dank and cold, and it smelled musty.

"Is this where we're going to live?" asked Anna.

"We'll stay here for tonight and see how it goes, OK?" I told her.

"Look, it's not so bad," said Liza. "Let's clean it up and see what we have down here."

"What did you all bring?" I asked.

They all brought some clothes and jackets. Anna had a small stuffed doll, and Anton had his toy soldiers and his toothbrush. Dmitry brought me my comics!

"We'll have to go back to the school for supplies," I said.

"You can't go back there. You'll get caught," said Natalia. "Can't we just go to town? It sounds quiet. Maybe they stopped the bombing."

"Even if they did stop, the soldiers are patrolling. They'll detain us or worse if they catch us," said Dmitry. "When do we go, Alex?"

"Liza, Natalia, can you straighten this place up a little while we go for supplies?" I asked.

"I can help too," said Anna.

"That would be great!" said Liza.

"What about us?" Anton asked about himself and Misha.

"Hey, look what I found," called Natalia. "It's a stove, and there's some coal in the bin."

I walked over to check. I had learned about coal from Papa when he made me take over running our furnace at home. There's a difference between anthracite coal and bituminous coal. Bituminous is a soft coal that's dirty to touch and to burn. It produces dark smoke and gasses.

Anthracite produces no smoke when it's burned and no dangerous gasses. We called it the good kind.

"Is it good coal?" asked Anton.

"Yes, it is. Good job Natalia. Anton, could you clean out the stove, and Misha, we'll need kindling to start a fire. Could you be sure it's dry, not green? I'll start the fire as soon as I get back."

"Ready?" I asked Dmitry.

"Let's do this. Should be a walk in the park compared to the rest of our day," he smiled.

CHAPTER 22

A Place to Call Home

We made our way back to the orphanage and crept around the outside of the wall to the back of the school. There was a space between the rusty panels that we knew we could squeeze through.

Once inside the grounds, we hurried to the side door next to the school entrance. We eased our way inside. There was no one around. The shelling had stopped, but they must have been waiting to be sure it was safe before coming back up from the shelter.

"You check out the laundry. I'll see if I can rustle up some food in the kitchen. I'll be right back," I told Dmitry.

"Make it fast. The staff will be coming back any minute," Dmitry whispered back.

I walked up the first set of stairs. The dorms were quiet. I continued up the second flight to the common rooms. I ambled through the dining room to the kitchen and started to look around for something to hold the food.

I found some bags under the sink along with several boxes of matches and some soap. I started filling the bags with bread, butter, a big chunk of yellow cheese. I didn't remember having this on the menu. It was probably for staff only.

In fact, I found lots of things that were not on our menu. It seemed the staff ate much better than the kids. I loaded up with smoked sausages, fresh vegetables, sweet cakes, and my favorite drink, lemonade.

"What are you doing here, boy!" It was Mrs. Bolin, the kitchen supervisor. She was in the dining room. She hadn't noticed the bags on the floor.

Think fast, Alex.

"Mr. Janko sent me up to check if it was safe, ma'am."

"I just got here myself. I was at my sister's visiting. She has a little farm just north of here. Lives there with her husband and children. It's a lot for her to handle, so I go to help out every couple of weeks…" *Is she kidding me? Why is she telling me all this?*

"Excuse me, ma'am. I should probably get back…"

"Oh yes, of course, sorry. I do go on when I'm

nervous. Well, everything here looks all right. I'll just go and check the stockroom to be sure."

As she walked past the kitchen door and down to the storeroom, I let out a breath of relief. If she had come into the kitchen instead of speaking over the serving area, she would have seen the bags of food.

I grabbed the bags and ran down the two flights of stairs to the laundry. Dmitry was waiting just outside the laundry door with a basket. I threw the bags on top and grabbed one side.

"You know we can't fit this through that little opening," I said.

"We'll just walk out the garden gate just like all guests do." Dmitry smiled.

And we did! Just like that, we were out the gate.

When we were clear, we stopped to catch our breath. We both fell to the ground laughing and cheering with relief.

"I can't believe we did it!" said Dmitry.

"We were just lucky," I retorted. "Could you imagine if Janko walked in and caught us?"

"After the beating you gave him? He probably

would've run away screaming!"

We lay there laughing. After a while, Dmitry said, "Well, dear, we had better get home and check on the kiddies."

***

Liza and the others had been working hard while we were gone. The cellar was mostly cleaned up and organized. There was even some furniture!

"Wow, how did you do all this?" asked Dmitry, clearly impressed.

"We went on a scavenger hunt through some of the other cellars. There's tons of stuff left in them!" said Anton.

"Allow me to give you a tour," said Natalia.

She walked over to the coal burning stove. "This is the kitchen."

Beside the stove was a square table with mismatched chairs. In the center of the table was a glass filled with wildflowers.

"I picked the flowers. Aren't they pretty?" Anna said proudly.

"They're beautiful," I commented. Anna beamed with pride.

A freestanding shelf stood against the wall to the right of the stove and held pots, some chipped and mismatched plates, and some cloudy glasses. On one end was an oil burning lamp casting light.

"Over here we have the parlor, complete with a rug!" said Misha.

"I found it all in the cellar right next door. I think it was the family's outside summer furniture. There aren't any cushions, but it's still pretty comfortable."

"And over here we have the bedroom. We found five cots. We're short by two, but we can take turns, right?" asked Anton.

I looked over at Liza. She stood there, beaming like a proud mama bird.

"This is like a miracle," said Dmitry. "I can't believe how much you did. It even smells better."

We all laughed because it wasn't the case. The cellar still smelled musty. But warming it up a little would help.

"Did you have a chance to clean the stove and get kindling? The only thing this place needs is a fire," I said.

"All set!" said Misha.

"OK, we did our part. How did you do?" smiled Liza.

I took the bags out of the basket. "Take a look," I said. "Tonite we feast!"

They squealed as they took inventory of our haul.

Dmitry dug into the basket and pulled out pillows, blankets, and even some underwear!

I stacked the kindling in the stove and topped it with some coal placed in the center. We found some old newspaper next to the stove, but it was too damp to light, so I dipped a few of the kindling pieces into the oil we had for the lamps. Soon the coal was red-hot and the cellar toasty warm. I had tended our coal furnace at home for years, so lighting the stove was second nature.

We lit the two lamps in the living room and bedroom sections. Next, we got out some food and started eating.

"I think we need to have a meeting to set up some rules," said Liza.

"I was thinking the same thing," I said. "We need to be very careful about giving ourselves away."

"I definitely don't think Janko or the others care enough to come after us, but we have to watch out for the military," said Dmitry.

"Dmitry's right. The protesters have become rebels, and they're fighting back. The soldiers are going to be expanding their patrol areas. We have to be careful not to leave any signs that we're here. We need to be sure the door is closed and locked all the time," I said.

"How will we get in if it's locked?" asked Anna.

"If none of us are here, it won't be locked. But if any of us are here, then we have to be locked in to be safe. We'll need to knock to be let in," I said.

"I know," said Anton. "A secret knock, like knock, knock, wait, knock, knock." He demonstrated on the table.

"I know another rule," said Misha. "No one goes out alone."

"Good one," said Natalia. "And we all have to know when someone does go out, and where they're going."

"We don't leave anything lying around outside," said Anna.

"The chimney shouldn't smoke now that the

253

coal's hot, but we'll need to keep it hidden, just to be on the safe side," I added.

"Tomorrow we need to find out what's going on in town," I said to Liza and Dmitry.

"Natalia and Misha, maybe you could find a source of water. I think there's a small lake close by, I don't remember exactly, but it could be a little north of here. Don't go too far. If you don't find it, we'll work out something else.

"Anna and Anton, could you finish checking out the cellars for anything else we can use? Make sure everything looks untouched. When you've finished, re-cover the doors with whatever growth covered them. Be on the lookout and don't leave the immediate area."

We straightened up and put the food away. We didn't have a refrigerator but the temperature that time of year was close to zero degrees Celsius, so I wrapped up the cheese and meat, put it in a box to protect it from critters and hid it outside.

"Who wants to get beaten at drunkard?" asked Liza. She was holding up a deck of cards, which she had pulled out of her backpack.

And so went our first night in our new home, temporary as it might be. We were happy in the here and now. Now we had food, and here we had shelter. Everything was great; we were free, we were safe, and we were a family.

CHAPTER 23

The Visit

The next morning I stoked the fire, grabbed some fruit, and sat down with Liza and Dmitry to plan our visit to town.

"We'll be going straight to the warehouse. I think we should backtrack on the same route we took to get out. Then we'll keep to the back alleys. We need to watch out for patrols and checkpoints," I said.

"Sounds good," said Dmitry. "Liza, you've never been to town, and you've never seen the things we've seen. I know you're older than I am, and you think you're supposed to be in charge—take care of me. But, you're gonna have to follow my lead on this one."

"Oh, sure…I understand." Liza smiled condescendingly. Her attitude made Dmitry angry.

"I'm not kidding around, Liza. If you want to come, you'll have to do things our way; if not, you can stay here and babysit!"

Liza was taken aback by his resolve.

"OK, Dmitry, I understand, honesty. I'll follow your lead on this one."

"Good. Let's get going. You guys remember everything we talked about last night?" I asked the other four.

"Yes, we do. Be careful, Alex." Anton gave me a quick hug.

"By the way Dmitry, we don't need a babysitter," he said with a scowl on his face.

He and Anna left to go rummaging for useful treasures. Natalia and Anton went looking for water, and we set out for town.

As we edged our way through alleys and behind buildings, we saw soldiers breaking up small groups of people before they could organize. They were none too gentle in their methods.

Trucks were filling up with dissidents who would be taken away to the makeshift prison at the armory. When one vehicle was full, another would take its place.

We noticed more roadblocks and made a mental note.

When we got to Kulbyshanka Street, it was full of soldiers and demonstrators who were facing off. The protesters began throwing rocks and bottles. That's when the soldiers moved forward with clubs and shields. Everyone started running in all directions. Those who tried to return with more projectiles were met with fire from the RCIDs.

Two protesters weren't fast enough, and as the RCIDs met their marks, both people caught fire. When others came to their rescue, gunfire forced them to retreat. Snipers started targeting the soldiers.

"We've got to get out of here!" I yelled to Dmitry and Liza. That's when I noticed Liza frozen in place with a look of sheer terror on her face.

"Liza!" I screamed. She didn't respond.

Dmitry grabbed her by the arms and shook her. "We've got to get out of here now, Liza!"

She snapped out of it and shouted, "OK."

We ran behind the building and across to the back of the warehouse.

When we entered, Vika and Mike were in the lunch room with Vlad having a meeting with some other men. They were shocked to see us. Mike stood and walked over.

"What the hell is wrong with you two? Why won't you stay away like we've told you over and over again?"

We had made it back through patrols, barricades, and rioting. I was calm and collected. But when Mike started towards me, I felt like the kid caught with his hand in the cookie jar and my "parental unit" was about to spank me! *Get it together. You don't take spankings or beatings anymore, remember?* I smiled to myself.

I gathered my courage, stood up as straight as I could, and looked him in the eye.

"No can do, boss. Our city's at war, and I have people in my life that need protection, too I…"

I looked at Dmitry and Liza. "No, *we* belong here."

He looked at me, looked over to Vika, then back to me. He just nodded his head and smiled.

"Why don't you wait up front. We'll be done here in a minute," said Vika.

Vlad nodded hello as we passed him.

We walked up front to the office. It was empty. I glanced around at the scorched walls and the broken windows, still covered in wood.

"What happened here?" asked Liza.

"What does it look like? There was a fire. I'm more interested in knowing what happened back there. Are you all right, now?" Dmitry was concerned.

"I don't know what happened, Dmitry. I just never thought it was like this. I know you told me, and I've seen the television reports, but up close, it's more heinous than I could have ever imagined." She was close to tears, but I could see that she was determined not to cry.

"I'm good now. I promise it won't happen again."

"Who is your friend?" Mike asked as he walked into the office.

"This is my sister, Liza. You remember her from Alex's party," said Dmitry.

"Oh yeah, of course. Good to see you again, Liza," Mike said. "Why don't we go into the lunchroom? Vika's finishing up now."

Vlad and the others left, and Vika came back in. He got us Cokes from the refrigerator and then joined us at a table.

"So, what's up?" he asked.

We told him what had happened when we got back to the school, and how we left with Anton and the others.

"Geez, kid, you think that was a good move? You know you can't stay here," said Mike.

"We already have somewhere to stay. It's safe, at least so far it is, and it's warm," I answered.

"Don't tell us where it is. Best if we don't know," said Vika.

"Why?" asked Liza.

"Just safer that way," answered Mike.

She looked confused but didn't say anything.

"We came to see what's going on, how much damage the mortar bombs caused. We also wanted to check the patrols and checkpoints, to see if they're getting closer to us."

"There wasn't too much damage. The shooters were aiming for the snipers in the abandoned apartment buildings. Now there's a mess!" said Mike.

"Yeah, we came in that way. Took a while to get through the rubble," I said.

"Didn't seem to stop the snipers. They were

shooting at soldiers when we got to town," said Dmitry.

"Did you see anything interesting with the patrols, any new checkpoints?" asked Mike.

"We noticed more patrols around Vyonoshka Street and more around the ruins, walking and driving," I said.

"You notice anything else; you let us know."

"Why?" Liza asked for the second time.

"Because we just like to keep informed. Can you say anything but why?" asked Mike.

She smiled. "Why?"

"You heading back now, Alex?" asked Vika.

"Yup."

"Here, take some Cokes for the others. How many more of you did you say?"

"Four."

***

We made it around the blockade that Dmitry and I had run into the day after the shelling by crossing Kulbyshanka Street at the warehouse and taking the alleys. We came out near my old school.

"Hey, Alex, didn't you tell me that you lived around here?" asked Dmitry.

"Yeah, right down that way," I said.

"Want to take a little detour and show us around?"

"Good idea, it'll be fun!" said Liza. "I'd love to see where the great Alex Krisko got his start."

I hesitated. Liza gave me her best pout and folded her hands as if in prayer.

"Damn. Come on, this way." I tried to sound irritated, but the truth was I felt a little excited at seeing the old neighborhood again. It had been quite a long time. I wondered if it had changed.

As we got closer to the house, I pointed it out.

"There it is, my old house. Hasn't changed a bit, just longer weeds."

I never expected to feel so nostalgic. Not so much sad as sentimental.

"I could see you and Anton living here. Nice," said Dmitry.

"Are we going to knock on the door?" asked

Liza.

I thought for a minute. "OK, but first I want you to meet someone."

They followed me as I walked over to Mrs. Babich's house. We walked up the stairs to the front door. I knocked. I was excited to see her.

The door opened slowly. "Yes?" Mrs. Babich asked peeking from behind the door.

"Hello, Mrs. Babich. It's me, Alex, from next door."

She opened the door a little wider and stared in disbelief. She stepped forward and placed her hand on my cheek.

"Alex, *moja doroha*, is it really you?"

She looked much older and frail.

"Yes, Mrs. Babich, it's really me."

She put her arms around me and began to cry.

"I prayed to see you once again before my time ends."

"Don't talk like that. You're still as young as I remembered," I lied.

She slapped my arm affectionately and laughed. "Always saying the right things. You look different, so tall and grown up." She noticed I wasn't alone.

"And who is this young man? Not Anton, surely!"

"This is my friend, Dmitry, and his sister, Liza." They both said hello.

"Come in, come in. It's cold out here. I'll make us a nice pot of tea. Where is Anton?"

"He's at home." She never asked where our home was. Maybe she didn't want to know the answer.

We sat, drank tea, and talked for a while. I told Mrs. Babich about Irina's call and how she and Paul had taken off. She said that she had heard from Mrs. Orlik that Irina and Paul were married and lived in Donetsk.

"Paul has gotten a job in one of the copper mines and is on strike," she said.

"Are riots going on there, too?" asked Liza.

"Yes, that's what I heard on the news. Probably worse than here," answered Mrs. Babich.

"Have you been next door to see your father?"

she asked me, concern in her eyes.

I placed my teacup on the table.

"Not yet. We're going there now. Have you seen him recently?"

"Not for a couple of weeks, but we don't socialize. Igor and I haven't spoken much since …" She stopped, took a deep breath, and finished her thought.

"Since he gave you to the state. Poor Yana, she must have turned in her grave. Such a good mother. She never would…"

I interrupted her. I didn't want to hear any more.

"We have to get going. Thank you for the tea. It was wonderful seeing you again."

"Please come back to visit, and bring Anton with you," she said as we shared a farewell embrace.

***

There was no answer at Papa's house. I was relieved. What if he were home, what would I say? What would he do?

I led Dmitry and Liza through the gate to the backyard. We passed the spot where Papa had

267

knocked Irina down with his fist. Memories began flooding back. Coming here was a terrible idea.

The back door was unlocked. I took a step in and called out. There was no answer, so I ventured in farther. No one was there. The house was a mess. It was obvious; no one had cleaned it since Irina left. It smelled like rotten food, cigarettes, and vodka.

We walked into the living room. There were old newspapers strewn around, cigarette butts everywhere, dirty glasses and empty bottles.

"It looks like it was a beautiful home at one time," said Liza.

"When Mama was alive," I answered.

As I walked around my old home, touching, remembering, the pain of my memories faded and in its place was a feeling of calm. I wasn't thinking about the bad things, just the good. I was finally coming to terms with my demons. I felt strong and unafraid.

"Let's see if there's anything here we can use, and then get back to the others. We've been gone long enough. Time to go home," I said.

CHAPTER 24

The Way of the Hunter

We got back and found the door locked from the inside. I smiled at Liza and Dmitry, who were also smiling.

"Who remembers the secret knock?" I asked.

"I think it was knock, wait, knock, knock, knock," said Dmitry.

"No," said Liza, "it was three knocks then wait." She smiled.

"And they call me 'smart ass.'"

I knocked twice, waited for a couple of seconds and knocked two more times. The door opened, and Anton stood there with a big grin on his face.

"What's the password?" he laughed.

"My brother's a dork!" I answered.

"Correct! You may enter."

We carried in the bags we took from Papa's house. We got an OK haul. Some more blankets, some canned goods, an ax, two hunting rifles and several boxes of ammunition.

Papa had never cleaned out our rooms or our closets, so I took Anton's old clothes. I thought something might fit Anna. I took all my old clothes for Anton, and maybe Natalia and Liza could find something that would fit.

Papa had two warm jackets hanging in the hall. I figured he must be wearing one if he was out, so I took them both. I also grabbed some of Mama's old books.

When Anton saw the things from Papa's house, he exploded!

"You went home without me? You had no right, Alex. It's my home, too! You had no right to go without me!"

"It wasn't his idea, Anton. We pushed him into it," said Liza. "He never planned to go, but then Dmitry remembered the house was somewhere close to where we were, and well, it just happened."

Anton glared at Liza. He was not ready to accept an explanation of any kind. He took one of Mama's books, went over to a cot, and sat down. I went over and sat next to him.

"I'm sorry, Anton. It was the wrong thing to do. But it's done now. What can I do?"

"Take me," Anton said, "Take me, or I'll go by myself."

"Don't even think about going there alone," I said.

"Then take me."

"You're so damn stubborn, Anton…OK, I'll take you, but I pick the time. Give me a few days to figure it out."

"He's super upset. Sorry, Alex, I didn't think," Dmitry said when I joined him at the table.

"Neither did I, and I should have. How am I going to take Anton to town? It's not safe. If he ever got hurt…" I just shook my head.

"He doesn't have to go to town, and you know that. Listen, we'll both take him as far as your old neighborhood and back. We should be able to make it that far without trouble," said Dmitry.

"You're right, we could. I'm just making excuses. I hate the thought of taking the kid out anywhere," I replied.

"He's not exactly a baby. You have to give him a little breathing room."

"I know, Dmitry, I know."

"Are you gonna tell him what Mrs. Babich said about your sister?" Dmitry asked.

"I don't think the timing is quite right. A) He just got over losing her. He hasn't brought her up since last Christmas. B) Like you said, he's super pissed at me right now. And C) he's very super pissed at me right now!"

"He's gonna be worse if he finds out from Mrs. Babich," said Dmitry.

"Yeah, you're right. I'll tell him before we go, just not tonight."

***

The food was getting low. We couldn't go to the school again. It was too dangerous. We had to think of something else.

"Let's go back to basics," said Dmitry, "the way it was done back when the Mongols were here and…" said Dmitry.

"You mean…starve like Mongol slaves?" Liza interrupted.

He rolled his eyes and gave her a sarcastic grin.

"Hunt. We've got your father's guns and ammunition. What have we got to lose?"

"Aren't you afraid they'll hear the shots and come searching for us?" asked Liza.

"There's shooting all over the city. A couple of little pops in the woods shouldn't draw any attention," answered Dmitry.

He did make sense in some ways. We had both been hunting at some point in our lives and knew how to use a gun, more or less. We did need food, and there was wildlife out there.

So, Dmitry and I decided to try hunting some brown hares, or maybe even some ducks over by the water.

On our first day out, we spent hours trying to find hares to shoot.

During the daytime, a hare will take cover in a depression called a "form" where he's supposed to be only partially hidden. Ha! They may as well have been ten feet underground 'cause we never saw a thing.

It was dusk, so we decided we better head back home. Just as we started walking, we saw one. A big brown hare going so fast, we nearly missed him. We tried to follow, but it was getting too dark.

"We better come up with something better than this," said Dmitry. "Let's go to the lake tomorrow.

If we can't shoot a duck, maybe we can catch a fish."

"Well, at least we know some hares are out there," I said.

"Very helpful to know if you can't catch one," laughed Dmitry.

"We might have to go to town soon, on a food run," I said.

"We better take Anton to your old neighborhood first, or he'll want to come. You don't want him going all the way into town, right?" asked Dmitry.

"Right," I said. "So when do you think? Tomorrow? The next day?"

"Let's stick to the plan and give hunting another shot at the lake, tomorrow; then we can take him visiting the day after," Dmitry answered.

***

We set off early the next morning with high hopes. We packed some food and some extra bullets and set off.

The lake was calming. We hid in the bushes and patiently waited to see if any ducks would come and set down in the water.

A few hours later, to our amazement, several ducks landed close to where we were hiding. We were very excited and nearly scared them away trying to get our rifles in place. Dmitry aimed, fired, and missed. The flock began to take off.

A fraction of a second later I fired, and Dmitry shot a second time. It was a miracle! One of the ducks fell into the water. It had a better chance of dying from a heart attack than getting hit by one of our bullets. But, there it was. We shouted and did a happy little hunting dance, slapping hands and wiggling our hips.

We ran to fetch our dinner. Dmitry beat me by a fraction and lay claim to it.

"I did it! I got a duck. I am a great hunter!" Dmitry held the bird up over his head as we stood in the water, waist deep.

"Are you kidding me? You scared the flock away when you tried to shoot that tree on the other side of the bank. This duck is my duck!" I joked.

"And yet, it's in my hands…my hands, my duck."

"OK, your hands, your duck. You can breast it," I laughed.

"Me? No, no, buddy boy. I shot it; you breast it.

That's how it works, you know, like if I cook, you do the dishes."

"In what universe?" The banter continued all the way home. We were wet and freezing, but we had a duck!

When we got there, Natalia and Misha were just coming back.

"Where have you two been?" I asked.

"Apple picking," said Misha. "We found an old orchard about half a mile in that direction." Natalia proudly showed us a shopping bag full of apples.

None of us knew a lot about cooking, just enough to get by. But that night we feasted on our version of the most delicious roast duck and baked apples ever made.

CHAPTER 25

The Unfortunate Encounter

"Let's go!" Anton demanded (for what seemed the hundredth time.)

It was time to satisfy my promise and take him back to the old neighborhood.

"Can Misha and I come along?" asked Natalia.

"Maybe next time," I answered.

"That's OK, Natalia," said Misha. "We planned to go fishing today, remember?"

"I'm going, too, but I'm not touching any icky worms!" said Anna.

We brought the hunting rifles along hoping to see some game on the way.

We took the route we had walked so many times before, delivering laundry. We went through the familiar trees and fields, but not as far up as Kulbyshanka Street. We decided to avoid all main streets by staying behind houses and cutting through yards. Soon we were back on our old street.

We were walking just a couple blocks from

Mrs. Babich's house. I guess we were feeling a little too comfortable, and we let our guard down. So, when a lone soldier came walking out from a backyard and onto the street, we never noticed until it was too late. We were just a few meters away from each other. He had already seen us and our rifles.

"Zupynjaty! (Stop!)." he yelled and started running after us while he attempted to get his handgun out of its holster.

We ran, but Anton wasn't fast enough.

"Alex!" I heard him scream and turned. The soldier had Anton by the collar. Anton was struggling to get free, making it hard for the soldier to get to his gun.

I was just about to rush to Anton's aid when Dmitry pushed passed knocking me to the ground. He got down on one knee and aimed his rifle at the soldier.

"Anton, get down!" he kept yelling until Anton threw himself to the ground. The soldier let go of him and released his gun from its holster. Just as he lifted his weapon, Dmitry fired. The soldier shot back. Dmitry's bullet hit the soldier in the leg. Even though the soldier was wounded, he began to raise his weapon a second time. Without thinking, I fired, and he dropped to the ground. Anton grabbed the gun off the ground and aimed it at the soldier.

I sprinted to him. In spite of the cold, sweat ran down my face and stung my eyes. I wiped my face on my shirt.

"Are you all right? Are you hurt?" I yelled as I ran. That was way too close. My heart was pounding.

I reached Anton, grabbed him by the shoulders and turned him, looking frantically for any sign of damage. He seemed fine.

I gently pushed his hand down; the gun was facing the ground. I reached down and put on the safety. He put it in his pocket, and I could tell he wasn't about to give it up without a fight. There just wasn't time for that now. So I let him keep the weapon.

I checked the soldier by shoving him with my foot. He didn't move. I wasn't sure what that meant, but I wasn't sticking around to see if he got back up. I had never shot anyone before. I should have felt terror, remorse, something. All I felt was relief that Anton wasn't hurt.

I looked at Anton. "Come on. We've gotta move."

He didn't stir. He was looking straight ahead. I followed his gaze, and I saw Dmitry sitting on the ground. He was bleeding! Anton hurriedly ran toward the friend who had just helped save his life. I followed.

"Where are you hit, Dmitry?" I asked.

"In my arm, and it hurts like a bi..."

"What are we gonna do?" interrupted Anton.

"We can't go to Mrs. Babich. She's too old to be put in this situation." I was thinking out loud.

I looked around and noticed that people had begun peeking out of their windows.

"We have to get to the warehouse, and we have to do it fast before soldiers begin to overrun this neighborhood."

***

The streets in town were busy with people whose only job, at the moment, was to provoke the soldiers, who must have been under orders to use restraint.

The *serzhant* (sergeant) stared at the people with hateful eyes, his jaw rippling, as his men stepped back from the crowd trying to avoid confrontation.

It won't last, I thought.

The commotion was distracting enough to get us past the crowds and to the warehouse.

We stormed through the back door.

"Mike! It's Dmitry; he's hurt!" I yelled.

Anton and I helped Dmitry to a chair as Mike came rushing over. He glanced at the rifles.

"What happened? Where are you hurt, kid?"

"I was shot in the arm."

Dmitry winced in pain as Mike slipped off his jacket.

"Alex, get the first-aid kit off of the wall over there." His voice was calm and professional.

Mike rolled up the sleeve of Dmitry's T-shirt to expose a bloody gash. He began to clean it so he could see what he was dealing with.

Vika came in. He was just returning from a meeting with his new chess buddy, *Molodshyl Leitenant* Benko. He looked at the guns, then at Anton and me, then at Dmitry's arm.

"How bad is it?" he asked Mike.

"The bullet barely grazed him. There's more damage to his jacket than his arm. A couple of stitches, and he'll be as good as new. Do we have any antibiotics left?"

Vika said they didn't. So he called Vlad, asked him to pick up a bottle from Dr. Holda and drop it off at the warehouse.

Mike finished bandaging Dmitry's wound. Then he made a sling out of a torn sheet, put it around Dmitry's neck, and eased his arm inside.

"Thank you," Dmitry mumbled.

Mike and Vika went to the other side of the room to talk. A few minutes later, they came over and sat down.

After what seemed an eternity, Vika spoke.

"Are you two the reason they're going house to house looking for the insurgents who are shooting soldiers on the street?"

"Can we explain?" I asked.

"Explain why you're walking the neighborhoods of Pervaiske with guns, shooting people? And in broad daylight. By all means, explain. I'm listening." Vika sat back and crossed his arms.

I started by telling him about the duck. At first, he rolled his eyes and took a deep breath. By the time I finished, it had made more sense.

"A very unfortunate encounter," said Mike.

"They have a description of all three of you, lucky it describes every kid in Ekrunia. Like Vika said, they're going door to door conducting searches.

"A lot of people are going to pay because you were nostalgic for the old homestead and decided it would be a good idea to carry rifles on the way." Mike paused. "Course you couldn't have known a member of the military would be that far from downtown."

"None of us could," said Vika.

"Do you know what he was doing there?" I asked.

"Probably visiting a girl," said Mike.

"Did we kill him?" asked Anton.

Mike could see that Anton was wrestling with his feelings. He sat down next to him.

"No, he's alive. Listen to me, kid. Even if he had been killed, there would have been nothing any of you could have done differently. If Alex and Dmitry hadn't shot him, one, maybe all three, of you would have been shot. You protected each other. That was the right thing to do."

Anton looked relieved, even grateful. He smiled at Mike.

Vlad came walking in with Danil and Eugene.

"Here you go, special delivery from Dr. Holda. The instructions are on the front of the bottle. And he said to give the extra bottle of antibiotics to you, Vika."

Vika went to put them away. Vlad was smiling.

"So, are these the new soldiers of the revolution?" he asked.

"Right now the only thing they are, are fugitives," said Vika as he came back in the room.

"I need to call on you again, Vlad. You're gonna have to work your magic and find a safe route out of here."

"Sure. Can't go until dark," said Vlad. "We'll be back around ten."

"Is everything arranged for tomorrow?" asked Mike.

"Going to finish up right now," Vlad answered and left with Danil and Eugene.

I looked over at Dmitry. I wondered if he was having the same thoughts. Were Mike and Vika more than just two businessmen? They said they had served together in the military. Were they somehow involved with the forces that were fighting the government?

"Are you with the opposition?" I blurted out without thinking.

Both Mike and Vika looked at me but didn't answer.

"Well, are you?" I repeated.

"Listen, kid," said Mike, "if we were in the, what did you call it, the opposition, then we wouldn't go around telling people, now would we?"

"Don't talk down to me, Mike. I want to know."

"Why do you want to know?" asked Vika.

"Because if you are, then I want to help."

"We want to help," corrected Dmitry.

"You're just kids," said Mike. "What could you do?"

"Plenty," said Dmitry. "We can sneak around unnoticed, deliver messages, report movements, and roadblocks...fight!"

"You think you could handle yourselves in a situation?" asked Vika.

"You mean like talking our way through a checkpoint? Or finding ourselves in the middle of a full-blown riot and getting out alive?" I asked.

"Or facing an armed soldier, shooting the bastard, and getting wounded in the process?" added Dmitry.

"You call that getting wounded? I've gotten worse scratches picking roses!" Mike teased.

"Seriously, guys. You both know what we've been through. We're tired of getting kicked around. Ekrunia is our country, too. We have a right to defend our freedom!"

Vika took a deep breath and blew it out slowly.

"OK... yes. We fight on the side of justice and freedom, just like your superheroes. But, unlike your superheroes, Alex, we can bleed. Our people are getting hurt, and worse, every day.

"Are you sure you want to be part of that? Once you're in, there's no going back."

"Yes."

"First things first. You'll need to stay away for a little while. At least until they give up looking for the three kids that shot an off-duty soldier. Then I'll give you a small assignment, and we'll see how it goes. I guess you'd better tell us where you live after all."

CHAPTER 26

A Surprise for Christmas

We knocked on the cellar door using our secret knock. Liza opened it and ran up the stairs.

"Where have you been? We've all been so worried!" she yelled. Her eyes were red and swollen from crying.

Then she saw the sling.

"Oh, my God, what happened?"

"Let us in. People are gonna hear you screaming all the way in town," said Anton. "Besides, we're freezing!"

We all went inside to escape the cold. It was warm and cozy.

Mike had given us some food to bring back with us. I handed the sack to Anna.

"Anna, could you take this?" I asked.

We put up our rifles. I turned and put my hand out to Anton. He knew exactly what I wanted. He reached into his pocket, pulled out the gun, and gave it to me. I placed it up on a ledge.

"What is he doing with a gun?" Liza asked me. Then to Anton, "Where did you get that?"

"Will one of you, please, tell us what happened?" yelled Natalia.

I told the story for the second time, leaving out the part about the duck.

"What was he doing so far from town?" asked Misha.

"Mike said he was probably visiting a girl," said Dmitry.

"Want some tea? We don't have milk, but it's hot," said Natalia.

***

We stayed close to home for the next couple of weeks. Dmitry's arm had almost healed. The seven of us spent all of our time together, walking, playing cards, and taking family outings to the river to fish. Thanks to Mike, Vika, and Mother Nature, we were doing well in the food department.

We spent hours talking about the opposition. We couldn't keep very well informed without a television or radio, but we could hear the shelling every night.

It was about a week before Christmas, and we decided that we were going to get ready to celebrate. Dmitry, Misha, Anton, and I found a tree and chopped it down. We dragged it back and set it up in the cellar. Liza, Natalia, and Anna picked greens to make wreaths and other decorations. We didn't have any string, but we found some vines to use for garland and for tying. When we finished, we looked proudly around our home.

"It's beautiful!" exclaimed Anna.

***

On Christmas morning, we decided to go for a walk. When we opened the door, to our surprise, it was snowing.

"What a wonderful Christmas!" said Anna. She twirled and tried to catch snowflakes on her tongue.

Then we heard a rustle in the woods.

"Quick, be very quiet and get back inside," I whispered.

Once inside, we bolted the door. We huddled together on the basement floor by the light of a single lamp. Suddenly, we heard footsteps above us. Someone was walking on top of the cellar. We waited. The footsteps stopped. I motioned to Dmitry. We slipped over to the table and got our rifles off the wall. We positioned ourselves between the door and the rest of our family.

Knock, knock, pause, knock, knock.

"Who the hell…?" whispered Liza.

"Anybody home?" It sounded like Mike, but we weren't sure.

I slowly went over to the door and listened. I heard a voice talking to someone. I released the metal bolt, stepped back, and waited.

"Surprise!" the voice hollered as the door flew open.

It *was* Mike. He was standing at the top of the stairs. When he saw the rifles aimed at him, he put his hands in the air.

"Whoa! Easy does it boys—it's just us. Think you could aim that in another direction?"

"Mike!" we all yelled at once.

Dmitry and I put our rifles back on the wall.

"It's OK. They're here. Come on in," Mike hollered over his shoulder.

Down the stairs came Vika, Vlad, and Mike. They had bags full of food and gifts.

I lit more lamps to brighten up the place.

"When you said you were living in a cellar, this is the last thing I would have imagined. It looks like a real home. Nice and warm, furniture, and you even decorated a tree!"

"I can't believe you're here!" said Anton.

Vika handed Anton a bag of food.

"Z Rizdvom! (Merry Christmas!)"

"Wow," Anton said and started pulling containers of food out of the bag. "Look at this! A real Christmas dinner, *holubtsi* (stuffed cabbage rolls), *vushka* (small dumplings with mushrooms), *borscht* (beet soup), and *kutia* (sweet pudding)! You brought *kutia!"*

Then he pulled out a bottle of vodka.

"That's for us big kids. Why don't you bring that right over here with a couple of glasses? There are Cokes and lemonade in there for you."

Mike and Vlad sat on the couch singing Christmas songs. We joined in while we set the table and warmed up the food. I felt as light as a feather, no orphanage, no Janko or Evanko. We were home safe, and we were celebrating Christmas together.

Vika was busy putting wrapped boxes under the tree.

Anton and Misha knew precisely where to get another table, so we added it next to the one we had. We brought over a couple of cots for extra seating, and Vika gave a blessing. We dug in.

We started with the soup. It was warm and sweet. The cabbage rolls were stuffed with real chunks of meat, not just rice like at the orphanage. We sat around the table moaning and smacking our lips. With each course, my clothes got tighter and tighter. We ate until we could barely move.

Then it was time for presents. We could hardly believe our eyes.

For Dmitry, a new soccer ball. For Anton and Misha, video games with extra batteries. For Anna, a new life-sized doll. Natalia and Liza got new sweaters with matching scarves.

And for me, new, never used Spiderman comics! There were ten of them, all protected by cellophane wrappers.

Vika, Mike, and Vlad sat there sipping their vodka and smiling.

***

It was late afternoon, and it would be dark soon. Time to go.

"Listen, before we go, we wanted to talk to you," said Vika. "We have a job for you. Vlad will give you the info, and I want you to come up with the detailed plan to make it happen."

"All of us," said Anna.

Vika, Vlad, and Mike looked over at me.

"I'll take care of it," I said. "I would never put her in danger."

"So, you're all in on this?" asked Vlad.

"All of us," said Misha.

"Who here can read a map?" asked Vlad.

Dmitry, Liza and I raised our hands.

"Step one, teach these kids to read a map. If they get separated, they'll have to find their way home."

Vlad opened a map and spread it out on the table.

"We have some friends who are being held illegally by the military. They're innocent civilians, not soldiers or fighters. We've arranged for them to be released (he made quotations with the first two fingers of each hand) in two weeks." I took that to mean they were escaping somehow.

"We need a plan in place to get them from point A, here, to point B, here, where another group will pick them up and take them to their final destination," said Vlad.

"You have a week to put your plan together, back it up with Intel, and run it by me," said Vika.

"Where do we get our Intel?" asked Dmitry.

"You get it yourselves. You pick the route; you check the route for troop movements, roadblocks, patrols, you name it. By the time we're ready to go you should know everything on and about your route, and be able to walk it blindfolded," answered Vlad.

"Any questions?" asked Mike.

"Looking at this map, I would guess a distance of about forty-eight kilometers is that about right?" Liza asked.

"Very good," said Vlad. "Forty-eight to fifty-six depending on your route."

"What time of day will we be traveling? Only at night?" asked Dmitry.

"Your call. Depends on the route and your Intel,"

"How many people, and what's the breakdown? Are they all adults?" I asked.

"Fifteen; twelve adults under the age of forty, three teens," answered Vlad. "Excellent questions."

He looked over at Mike and Vika. "This just might work," he said.

CHAPTER 27

A Sick Friend

We didn't have much time to get a plan together. We had no experience at war, but we were determined to do a good job. Fifteen people would be depending on us to get them to a safer place. Mike and Vika would be depending on us.

Liza, Dmitry, and I took turns teaching the others how to read a map. We concentrated on deciphering the map Vlad gave us. We could get into more map reading detail after the mission.

Initially, guns weren't supposed to be part of our mission. Maybe Vika or Mike thought we weren't ready. But that position didn't last. Even though we were subversives and had to go undetected, or the task could be in jeopardy; we needed to protect ourselves and our charges. So it was decided we would have weapons with us.

We all needed to be trained in weapons, (even though we only had the two rifles) and we needed to be trained fast. Mike volunteered.

Eventually, we would have to get more weapons somewhere. Maybe Mike could help us out if we did well on this mission.

And then there was Anton, who insisted the handgun belonged to him. I couldn't have him shooting himself by accident, so he had to learn to use a gun, too. Or, more important, when not to use one.

***

We made the trip ourselves, making notes of any military activity. We saw two checkpoints that we would have to go around, so we found alternate routes and marked the maps accordingly.

When we made it to the farmhouse that was marked point B on the map, we didn't approach it, just made notes, and went back into the woods where we planned to camp for the night.

We had packed enough food, but it was colder than we thought it would be. We couldn't light a fire, couldn't risk it being seen. So we spread a blanket on the ground, put the younger ones in the middle and snuggled as close as we could. Then we placed another blanket over us.

The ground was frozen, and the chill crept through. The blanket covering us did little. We barely slept.

When it began getting light, we got up and started the long trek home. On the way back, we double-checked our facts.

It took us close to eleven-and-a-half hours to get back. We made a note of the time.

The first thing I did when we got back was light a fire in the stove to warm up. We were chilled to the bone. We were all so tired. We grabbed a bite to eat and went to bed. I slept nearly twelve hours!

I was the first one to wake up. I put more coal on the fire and put some water on for tea. Liza got up next, then Natalia, Misha, Dmitry, and Anton. Anna was still sleeping.

We tried to figure out what to have for breakfast. I went outside to look in our "refrigerator." We had some leftover sausage and five eggs. We decided to scramble them so they would stretch enough to feed all of us.

When breakfast was ready, Liza said, "We should wake Anna."

"I'll do it," said Anton. He hopped out of his chair and ran over to her cot.

"Time to get up," he said while shaking her gently. "Breakfast is ready."

"I'm not hungry," said Anna, and she turned over to go back to sleep.

"Poor thing, she must be exhausted," said Natalia.

We finished breakfast, cleaned up, and went back to work on our plan. We worked outside and took turns at shooting.

Around one, we went inside to eat lunch and warm up.

"Anna is still sleeping," said Liza, with an edge of concern in her voice.

She walked over and woke her up.

"Hey, honey. Are you all right? Are you hungry?"

"Hi, Liza. No, I'm just so tired and cold," she answered sleepily.

Liza felt her forehead. "You feel a little warm. I'll let you rest. We're right here if you need anything."

Anna got up mid-afternoon. She still didn't want to eat, but she joined Anton in a game of drunkard. After one game she got tired and went back to bed.

We still had two days before we had to present our plan to Mike and Vika. We were feeling pretty confident but went over it again and again. It had to be perfect. After that, we joined Anton for some cards, took a break for supper, and played more cards until we went to bed.

**

The next morning, Liza woke me.

"It's Anna," she said. "She's burning up with fever."

I jumped up off the couch where I slept and went over to her. She was very groggy. I touched her forehead, and she felt as though she were on fire. By now, everyone was up.

"What are we going to do for her? She's very sick!" said Liza. "Should we take her to Mrs. Babich?"

"No, not there, the patrols, remember?" I said.

"What about Sophia and Daniel?" Anton asked.

"That's a pretty good idea," I answered.

Everyone knew about Sophia and Daniel and how they cared for Anton and me. We had told them dozens of stories over time. They all agreed that's where we should take Anna.

"We have to figure out how we're going to get her there. She can't walk," said Natalia.

"Would a wagon work?" asked Misha. "I saw a toy wagon in the cellar next door. Maybe we could rig up a seat of some kind to hold her."

We wrapped Anna in blankets, made a seat in the wagon with pillows, and placed her in it.

She was half-sitting, half-lying. As soon as she was in, she went back to sleep.

"Should we come with you?" asked Dmitry.

"No, we'll be fine, thanks."

"I'm coming!" said Anton.

"I know. I wouldn't even try to stop you," I said.

We couldn't walk as fast as we wanted to because Anna wasn't very stable and we didn't want her to fall out.

We finally arrived at the house. I walked up and knocked on the door. After a minute, Sophia answered. She looked shocked to see me.

"Hi, Sophia. I need your help."

She stepped forward and put her arms around me. I felt so excited to see her. I hadn't realized how much I missed her.

She released her hold on me and looked straight ahead.

"Anton?"

He smiled back at her but wouldn't leave Anna's side.

"Sophia, we have a sick friend, Anna. We didn't know where else to go."

"Quickly, bring her in," said Sophia.

I carried Anna into the house and laid her down on the couch. Sophia checked her, then told me to get the thermometer out of her bathroom cabinet.

Her temperature was nearly 103° F!

"I'm going to put her in a bath and try to get the fever down. You wait here. Get something to eat or drink while you wait."

Sophia came back an hour later.

"She's resting in your old room. I gave her some medicine for the fever and a bath. Her temperature's down some for now." She sat down on a chair across from us.

"I think it's time to fill me in," said Sophia.

We talked for more than an hour about what had

happened since we left her.

"I am so sorry you went through all that." She had tears in her eyes.

"This cellar you live in—is it the reason Anna is so sick?"

"No, I'm sure it isn't. It's warm and dry, and we keep it very clean." Anton assured her. "And we eat good food. Our friends Mike and Vika make sure."

I suddenly realized how quiet the house was.

"Where are the kids?" I asked.

"They all moved on some time ago," Sophia answered. "The state found Michael and Yana's grandmother living in Crimea. They went to live with her. Tanya and Sasha were both adopted by American families."

"Some stories do have a happy ending. I'm so glad for all of them." I felt warm thinking about them.

"When will Daniel be home? We were hoping to see him before we have to leave to get Anna home."

"She really shouldn't be taken back out in the cold. Why don't you leave her here for a few days, until she's well."

"Are you sure?" I asked. "We don't want to cause you any trouble."

"It's no trouble. You should know that. I'll do anything I can to help you both and your friends, too" she said.

"Thank you, Sophia. Well then, I guess we'll head back as soon as Daniel gets home."

Sophia looked down at her hands. She folded them tightly as if trying to prevent them from trembling.

"He won't be back for some time. In fact, I don't know how long he'll be gone. He was arrested as a dissenter. He tried to intervene when he saw a young girl being harassed by two soldiers."

I was shocked!

"Where is he being held?" I asked.

"At the armory. But they only keep people there for a few weeks, and then they transfer them to prisons." She began to cry. My heart broke for her.

Anton looked over at me. I gave him a signal to be quiet.

"We have to go," I told her. "It's gonna be all

right. Daniel's a good man. I'm sure they won't keep him long."

She wiped her eyes and smiled. "Anna will be okay. Why don't you see if she's awake so you can say good-bye? Tell her you'll pick her up in a week or so."

CHAPTER 28
A Special Payback

When we got home, we told everyone that Anna would be staying with Sophia for a while, but she'd be okay. Then we told them about Daniel.

"We have to do something. We can't let him go to prison!" said Anton.

"What can we do?" asked Dmitry.

"I had a thought," I said. "Tomorrow when we go into town to give Mike and Vika our plan, I'm going to tell them that they have to include Daniel in the release."

"Tell them?" Liza questioned. "Wouldn't it be better to ask?"

"Ask, but insist at the same time," said Dmitry "We'll back you, right?" He looked around the room. Everyone agreed.

The next day, we all made the trek to the warehouse. I was on pins and needles the entire trip.I kept rehearsing over and over in my head what I would say to Vika and Mike.

You have to get him out, or we won't go! Too

forceful. Besides, we had to go. I couldn't make them so mad that they kicked us out.

Please, is there any way you can get him out, for us? Too wishy-washy. That's how a kid would ask. I was trying to earn respect as a man.

I went on that for more than an hour until we walked into the warehouse.

Mike, Vika, and Vlad were waiting in the empty lunchroom. There weren't many employees left. They were either afraid to come into town or had left the city of Pervaiske. Not many orders for rentals were coming in any way. The hospital was the only one that still needed deliveries. Vika had just enough employees to keep them supplied.

He had made a deal with *Polkovnik* Kogut, who was in charge of the occupation. It allowed Vika's trucks to keep making deliveries within the city limits. Colonel Kogut's injured men were treated at the hospital, so he could hardly refuse. After that, Vika and the colonel became chess buddies, or so the Colonel thought, and Vika had more freedom to come and go than anyone in Pervaiske.

We got right down to business. I spread out the map Vlad had given us.

"Dmitry, Liza, you go first," I said.

"Thanks," said Dmitry. "We'll be making the first part of the trip in the dark. We meet up here, at three a.m. You turn over the civilians, and we head out. There are checkpoints here and here, so we'll leave town by going due west, through the cornfield here. Past there, we didn't see any troops until we got to the edge of the Malkovia preserve—here."

"They have a camp set up," said Liza.

"And," I added, "we spotted a scouting unit here. We'll detour northeast for a couple of kilometers, to avoid that area. But there's no way to tell when or where we'll see another one."

"Guys?" I nodded towards Misha and Natalia.

"That's where we come in," said Natalia. "We scout ahead of the group and if there's any new activity we report back to Dmitry and Alex."

"If anyone sees us, then we're just a couple of kids playing a little too far from home," said Misha.

"We made it to the field by the farmhouse in less than twelve hours with no stops. There aren't any streams or rivers on this route, so each person should carry some water, maybe a little something to eat," I finished.

"We'll give them what they'll need," said Mike.

"Good job," said Vika. "Now, don't take this

the wrong way. This mission will be your very first, and I have faith that it'll be a successful one. But I'm sending Mike along, just to observe. It's still your mission."

I nodded.

OK, get ready, it's now or never. Ask. I suddenly had the jitters. *Don't shake! Keep it together!*

"Mike, Vika? I need to talk to you about something," I said. "It's important."

"Is it about the mission?" asked Vlad as he stood to leave.

"Yes, it is," I said.

"Stick around a minute, will you Vlad?" asked Vika.

"Do you remember me telling you about our foster parents, Sophia, and Daniel?"

"Sure. Why?"

"Anna got sick, she's going to be OK, but we took her to Sophia."

I went on to tell them how Daniel was arrested and being held at the same place as the civilians they were getting "released."

"This is important to me, Mike, Vika." I looked from one to the other.

"I can't just leave him there after everything he did for Anton and me."

Vika looked around the room at us, then over to Vlad and Mike. I waited with bated breath.

"It's kind of late in the game to make changes said Vika. My heart dropped.

"We might be able to do something; it is just one more. I can't make any promises, but we'll do our best to make it happen. We have five days before the mission. One of us will come to you, the day after tomorrow." Vika smiled.

***

"You were quiet back there," I said to Anton on the way home. "What's going through your mind?"

"You said it all, brother. You did much better than I could have. I'm too emotional when it comes to Sophia and Daniel. Do you think they'll get him out?"

"Yes, I have to. I can't stand to think of the alternatives. We'll have to tell Sophia the minute we hear from Vika that it's a go."

***

We were having target practice when we saw Vlad coming towards us. We shouldered our guns and walked out to meet him.

"Hope you have some good news for us," I said as we shook hands.

"I'm too cold to talk. You have any of that vodka leftover from Christmas?"

"Well, we sure didn't drink it! Come on back to the cellar. We'll set you up."

Vlad sat on a chair at the kitchen table. "I still can't get over how comfortable you've made this place for yourselves," Vlad said as I handed him a glass of vodka.

"So, what's the news?" I was anxious and too impatient to wait for him to drink, but he put the glass to his mouth. He took a long sip.

"It was a problem at first, but a little money changed hands, and it looks like Daniel Kozel will be released along with our other friends."

We all shouted with relief!

Vlad took one last gulp of his drink and said, "Let's go over the plan one more time."

I got the map and spread it out.

"We meet here at three in the morning. We now have sixteen going," said Vlad.

"Seventeen," I interrupted. He looked at me quizzically. "Sophia, Daniel's wife." Vlad let out a big sigh.

"I'll let Vika know. How are you going to get her there? We can't risk her getting picked up for wandering the streets and breaking curfew at three o'clock in the morning."

"You're right. I'll take care of it," I said

"I'm going to walk back with Vlad," I told Anton when we were finished going over the plan. "I want to see Sophia."

"I'm coming," said Anton. He stood up and grabbed his coat.

I was stressing out about Daniel, Sophia, the mission…Anton's stubborn assertiveness rubbed me the wrong way.

"Listen up! If you want to be a part of this unit, then you had better learn to take orders. You can't just dictate what you're gonna do!" I snapped.

He looked like I had just punched him in the stomach. The room went silent.

"Walk with me," Vlad said under his breath.

When we got outside, he looked at me and said, "What was that all about? If you want to lead this ragtag group, you can't be going off on them like that."

"I know. It's never happened before, and it won't happen again," I said. "I'm worried about Anton's stubborn streak. If he gets something in his head while we're on a mission…"

"Tell him that. Don't single him out in front of the others. Be respectful enough to sit him down and talk to him.

"I'm gonna get going. You need to talk to Anton…now." He shook my hand and smiled. Then he slapped me on the back and left.

I decided to have my talk with Anton in front of the group. If I had embarrassed him in front of them, then I needed to apologize in front of them as well.

I went back inside and bolted the door.

"I need to apologize to all of you for my outburst, but especially to you, Anton. It was wrong of me to shout at you like that, and you have my word, it won't happen again. I'm sorry."

Anton paused for a minute and then said, "So what you're saying is that you won't yell at me again."

"Yes, Anton. That's what I'm saying, and I'm sorry it happened today."

"Never, no matter what I do?"

"Well, I didn't say that exactly."

"Like, what if I tell Liza that you like her, and you think she's beautiful, you won't do anything?" He smiled that same mischievous smile I had seen on Dmitry so many times.

"That's ridiculous!" I retorted.

"That I'm beautiful?" Liza said with a pout.

"Yes! No! I mean you *are* beautiful, but—"

They all burst out laughing.

"Better quit while you're ahead, buddy," said Dmitry. My face felt hot.

"Seriously, though, you were right in a way," said Dmitry. "Someone has to have the last word if this is going to work. I nominate Alex. All in favor?"

They all raised their hands.

"That's five yes votes. You are officially in charge."

"Then I officially name you my second-in-command." I smiled at Dmitry, relieved at the change of subject.

"You know what? We still have plenty of daylight. Why don't we all go and visit Anna? Then Dmitry and I will talk to Sophia. You're welcome to sit in, Anton." He smiled at me.

***

Sophia was glad to see us, but Anna squealed with delight when we walked into the house. She was lying on the couch watching a video, her face was still a little flushed, and she had a mean cough.

"How is she doing?" I asked Sophia.

"She's still running a little fever, but she is improving every day. She's eating better, and she's in excellent spirits. I'm going to make everyone some hot chocolate. How does that sound?"

I went into the kitchen to help.

"This visit is perfect for her. She keeps asking when you're coming. She's anxious to go home. But I have to be honest, Alex. She's not ready to go. I think her fever should break in a day or so. I'd like to keep her until then," Sophia told me.

We took the hot chocolate into the living room. Sophia put out a plate of cookies to go with it. After a few minutes, I couldn't contain myself any longer.

"Sophia," I began, "I have some news about Daniel."

She looked puzzled. "How do you have news about Daniel?"

"We have friends. You have to swear on your life, and Daniel's that this goes no further than the people in this room." She agreed hesitantly, still not sure what I was telling her.

"OK. Hear me out, and then you can ask anything you want.

"A group of sixteen people will be escaping from the armory the day after tomorrow. Daniel will be one of them. We'll be escorting them to Novopski. There another group will take over and escort them north to safety. We can take you, too, but you have to leave everything behind, at least until this is over and martial law ends. Once the soldiers leave, it'll be safe for you to come back."

"Are you telling me the truth? You're children, how can you do this?"

Sophia looked more confused than before.

"We're young. We're not children anymore Sophia, not after all we've been through together. We work with the opposition. It's already been arranged. If you want to be with Daniel, you'll need to do everything we say. Can you trust us that much?" I felt confident and in control.

"To be with my Daniel again, yes, I'll do whatever you say," she responded.

"Good. Anna, honey, I'm sorry, but you'll have to sit this one out. You're still sick, and it's going to take more time for you to get well," I told her.

"We're going to take you to a very nice lady who will take care of you until we get back. You can't tell her anything you heard today. Swear?"

She held up her pinkie finger. Liza reached over and did the little ritual that goes with pinkie promises. I guessed that made it legitimate.

"We'll pick you up tomorrow morning. Anton, Dmitry, and I will take you there. Her name is Mrs. Babich. She's very sweet, and she just as nice as Sophia. I know you'll love her.

"Liza, Misha, and Natalia, while we take Anna to Mrs. Babich, you'll take Sophia back home with you. Sophia, take only what you can carry for a long distance. Both of you should be ready to go by nine in the morning. Any questions?"

There were none.

CHAPTER 29

A Special Dinner

Sophia and Anna were ready to go when we arrived. Sophia had dressed Anna in warm clothes and given her some medicine. She handed me the bottle.

"This is what I've been giving Anna for her fever. Give it to your friend, Mrs. Babich," said Sophia.

"Thank you," I said. "Are you ready to go?"

"I can't believe I'm doing this. When will I be with Daniel?"

"The day after tomorrow. Are you sure you want to go through with this?"

"I don't know what I'm doing here; why I'm turning my fate over to someone so young. But, for some reason, I trust you, Alex.

"Yes, I'm sure."

"Liza's made this trip many times," I said. "Misha and Natalia know what they're doing, too. Follow their lead, and you'll be safe. You should be there in an hour. Do you have everything?"

"Whatever I can carry for a long distance." She

smiled.

***

Since the shooting, the unfortunate incident, soldiers were patrolling everywhere in the old neighborhood. There was just no way to get around it. The only way to get Anna to Mrs. Babich was to walk right through.

We headed to the school, which was still open in spite of the fighting. With a bomb shelter beneath the school, it was thought to be the safest place for the kids to be.

The plan was to have Anton walk Anna to Mrs. Babich's house. The story was that Anna was Anton's little sister, and they were coming from their school where Anna had gotten sick.

Dmitry and I found a safe spot to watch them walk. We could see nearly all the way down the street.

We went over the story one last time, and I sent them off.

The minute I saw them approaching the street, I had second thoughts. *What if the guards don't buy their story? They wouldn't hurt little kids.* I tried to reassure myself. My heart began racing.

I watched as a patrol approached them. Anton had

his arm around Anna like a loving brother. The men exchanged words with Anton and Anna, and then I was relieved to see them wave the kids on their way.

I expected that it would take Anton at least half an hour to return. He would want to visit for a minute with Mrs. Babich. I gave him strict orders not to go next door to Papa's house.

It had been nearly an hour. I was beginning to panic. What could be taking so long? Something must have gone wrong.

"Dmitry, it's been too long. We have to go and get him." I tried not to let my fear show.

"Give it five more minutes. If something went wrong, we would have heard shouting or something." Dmitry sounded much calmer than I felt.

Finally, we saw a little speck of a boy coming down the street. As he got closer to us, the soldiers saw him and waved at him. I heard him yell, *"Djakuju vam, panove.* (Thank you, sirs.)"

He crossed the street and walked to the back of the school. When we caught up with him, I grabbed him and held on to him for dear life!

"I can't breathe, Alex!"

I let him go, stood back and just looked at him,

thankful he was safe.

"I did it, guys! I thought I would get scared and blow it, but I remembered that you and Anna were counting on me, and I wasn't scared at all!" He was beaming with pride. So was I.

We headed straight home. On the way, Anton filled us in on his visit.

"Mrs. Babich was shocked to see me. She said I had grown a foot and that I looked just like you, Alex. I said 'No way, I'm much better looking!'"

"Ha-ha, you wish you were half as good looking as I am. What did she say about taking care of Anna?"

"She's happy to do it. I told her that Anna's folks had been arrested, and she's staying with us. Then I told her that Anna got sick, but we didn't know how to take care of her. She's gonna tell everyone that Anna is her grand-niece and she'll be staying there for a while because the government is holding her parents. I told her we'd be back in about a week," said Anton.

"Didn't she ask where we live?"

"No, she didn't. I figured you must've told her something when you were there," he answered.

"Good work!" said Dmitry.

We got home late afternoon. It had been a tiring, but good day. We knocked on the cellar door, and as soon as it opened, the scent of *holubtsi* filled our nostrils.

"Please tell me that's cabbage rolls I smell," said Dmitry, sniffing the air as he walked down the stairs.

The table was all set up for supper, and delicious looking food covered our little heating stove.

"Where did all this come from?" I asked. The delicious smells were making my stomach growl.

"I couldn't leave it in the refrigerator," said Sophia. "The house will be locked up until Daniel, and I go home. Why let good food spoil?"

"Sophia's a miracle worker. She cooked all this on our little stove!" said Natalia. "Wait till you see what else she made for us."

"*Verhuny*!" Natalia exclaimed.

"No way," said Anton. "Angel wings? That's my favorite!"

"I know," smiled Sophia. "A little bird told me a long time ago."

***

The time passed quickly, and soon it was time to

go. We had spent hours getting ready for this mission. We were as prepared as we could ever be. Vika and Mike made sure of that. Dmitry and I filled our pockets with the last boxes of bullets.

Anton took the handgun he had procured from the unfortunate incident and put it in his backpack.

Safety on?" I asked him.

"Not an idiot!" he said without looking at me.

"I know. Sorry."

He smiled. Out of the corner of my eye, I saw Dmitry smiling.

Sophia saw us from the stairs. She glanced at the guns but said nothing. When I looked over at her, she was watching us with a grin and an expression of…what? Wonder? Amazement?

Respect, I thought. *That's what it is, respect.*

Without warning, I was filled with nostalgia and an overwhelming affection for my foster mother. I walked over to her, and we embraced.

"Thank you for doing this," she whispered in my ear.

"You saved us once. Time to return the favor. Ready?"

She nodded.

We had to get just over three kilometers north of the ruins downtown to a barn where we would meet up with Mike and the others. We traveled straight north from home then west. We arrived a little early.

"Where are they?" asked Sophia. "Something must have gone wrong." She had tears in her eyes and a look of sheer panic.

"Nothing's gone wrong, I promise. We're early. They'll be along any minute."

I was trying to convince both of us.

"You sure?" whispered Dmitry.

"I'm sure that I hope so," I answered.

Five minutes went by, then ten. Still no sign. Misha was watching for them by the road.

After nearly fifteen minutes of holding my breath, Misha rushed into the barn.

"They're coming! I saw Vika's truck," he said.

I ran out. It *was* Vika's truck.

"Hurry! Open the doors!" I yelled.

The barn doors flew open just as the truck turned

off the road and drove directly into the barn. We closed them quickly.

Mike got out of the truck and gave me a quick handshake. Then he pulled me in for a hug and a slap on the back.

"Where's Vika? I asked.

"He went ahead to firm up on the other end," he answered.

We walked around to the back of the truck and opened the doors. Out came our charges, one by one, looking relieved and frightened at the same time.

The last to exit was Daniel. He stopped in his tracks, looking shocked when he saw his wife. Before he could say a word, Sophia came running and threw herself at him. They embraced and cried while Anton and I looked on.

"Sophia, what are you doing here?"

Then he saw Anton and me. "Can someone please tell me what's going on?" said Daniel, trying to compose himself.

"Later," I said, "when there's more time. We need to go."

I started to walk away. Then I turned.

"Good to see you again, Daniel."

CHAPTER 30

The Road to Freedom

"OK, everyone, please line up over here." Mike paused while everyone complied.

"This is Alex, Anton, Dmitry." He walked past each of us as he said our names. "Liza, Natalia, and Misha. They'll be in charge from here to the rendezvous point in Novopski."

"What the hell is this, kids?" yelled one of the men. The others joined in to protest.

"Hold on!" shouted Mike. "They're card-carrying members of the opposition!"

"I got this," I told Mike.

"OK, kid." He stepped back. I held my hands in the air to quiet the crowd. When they finally complied, I began.

"I get it. To you, we look like a bunch of kids. Yeah, we're young, but in spite of our looks, my crew and I are trained professionals working for the opposition. We know this mission inside and out and can get you safely to Novopski. We've worked with Mike and Vika before, and they wouldn't trust us with your safety if we couldn't get the job done.

Now, we're wasting precious time. We have to be far from here before sunrise. If you want to come, get your things and follow us, we're leaving now."

Liza and Dmitry took the lead. As the line began to follow, Mike pulled me aside and murmured, "Professionals? Laying it on a little thick, aren't we, kid?" he teased.

"Just get in line before I leave you behind to fend for yourself," I teased back. "Watch and learn, old man."

***

By mid-morning, we had covered more than half our distance with no sign of troops. We had walked seven hours straight, and I was pleased with our progress. I decided to give everyone a break. I picked a serene spot in the woods.

"We'll be stopping here for fifteen minutes. Rest up and have something to eat. Mike brought some sandwiches.

"Mike, if you want to give them to Anton, he'll pass them out." I turned to Dmitry.

"See if you can catch up to Misha and Natalia. Have them come in for a break. Liza, you and I will guard the perimeter while they rest. Why don't you grab a sandwich and take it with you?"

While I was on guard, Daniel approached me.

"Sophia filled me in. You've grown up since I last saw you." He seemed a little ill at ease.

"Look, this is a great thing you're doing. I don't know how to thank you."

"No need to thank us, Daniel. We owe you." He smiled at me.

"Sophia and I, well, we've decided to continue the fight in Kirovsk. Do you know where that is?"

"Sure, north-west of where we're going," I said.

"Sophia's uncle had a farm there before he passed away. He bequeathed it to Sophia's mother, who left it to her. It's just sitting there, growing weeds. The house is empty, probably falling apart. We'll know when we get there.

"We spoke with Mike, and he's going to arrange for us to meet with Vika Burick. We're going to set up a safe house. You got us thinking about where we stand on all of this. I want to thank you for that, too. If any of you ever need our help, you've got it, no questions asked."

I nodded, and he walked back to Sophia. She looked up at him with so much love; it warmed my heart just to see them. I felt—I don't know—proud.

I called Liza in and walked over to Natalia and Misha.

"How are you doing?" I asked.

"Good," they both answered.

"It's been clear so far," said Misha.

"Good," I replied. "OK, back to work. Go, relieve Dmitry. It's time we get going. Don't take any unnecessary chances out there. You see anything out of the ordinary, get back to us, pronto."

They left, and we started back out on our journey. A few minutes later, Dmitry came back and joined the group.

Mike and I were in the lead, and we thought we heard voices. Dmitry, Anton, and Liza were in the back. I stopped and raised my hand signaling for everyone else to stop. Mike and I listened; we heard it again. Mike pointed in the direction of the voices. They were coming from the woods. We were in between patches of forests in a field, wide open! All we could do was to make a run for it and hope whoever it was would be too busy to notice.

Mike and I motioned for everyone to move as quietly as possible. As Dmitry and Liza herded the group to safety, we stayed behind to make sure they made it. They were nearly there when we saw who the voices belonged to. It was a scouting unit of about five government soldiers. Just as they got to the edge of the woods, they spotted the group.

"Ostanovyt! (Stop!)" one of the men yelled in Russian.

Mike and I dropped to one knee in the tall grass and opened fire. The soldiers hadn't noticed us yet. Before they figured out where the shots were coming from, two of them were down.

I spotted Anton. He had his handgun and was hiding behind a tree, firing. Mike and I tried to run while Anton kept them busy. No good. The three of them split their fire between us. We hit the dirt. I put my head up to aim just in time to see one of the soldiers take a bullet. I looked over at Anton. He was behind the tree reloading his gun.

Again, I aimed and began firing. Mike was a few feet to my left. Another one fell.

"Hold fire!" screamed Mike. Anton slid farther behind the tree and waved in acknowledgment.

I looked over at Mike.

"Why did you tell us to stop shooting?" I knew there was at least one more soldier over there.

"I thought I saw…"

There was another shot, and the last soldier fell to the ground. But none of us had fired!

Then I saw Dmitry. He had circled around and come upon them from the back. He walked up to each of them, taking their guns and checking for vitals. We stood up.

"I knew I saw someone back there firing," said Mike.

"Anton," I hollered, "you and Liza check to be sure everyone's OK."

We rushed over to Dmitry. "Great move. Did you learn that watching John Wayne movies from America?" I said.

I could see by the look on his face that he was as scared as I was. What were we doing out in the woods in a gunfight? We both laughed at the absurdity of it all.

"Someone must have heard all that shooting!" interrupted Mike.

"You're right. Help me hide these guys and then

let's get the hell out of here!" I said.

Everyone was unhurt. We rushed on, hoping to leave a lot of distance between us and anyone who might have heard the shooting and decided to investigate.

After a few minutes, we slowed down a little.

There were three teens in our group. One was a girl who looked sickly and frail, but managed to keep up the pace with everyone else. When we slowed, the altercation must have hit her because she began shaking and crying uncontrollably as she walked. Liza walked over to her.

"Hi, I'm Liza. Are you doing all right?"

"I'm fine," she said between hiccups. "I can keep up."

Liza went back to her position. Anton decided it was his turn to talk to the girl.

"I'm Anton. What's your name?"

"Maria."

"Boy, Maria, did you ever see anything like that? I've never been so scared in my life. Look, I'm still shaking." He shook himself uncontrollably from his head to his feet. She stopped to watch him curiously.

When he had finished, he said, "There, I feel better. Wanna try?"

She laughed while she mimicked Anton's performance.

"Keep up," I smiled as I picked up my pace and passed them.

I caught up with Mike and Dmitry at the front of the line. Mike didn't look quite right. He was pale.

"You OK, Mike?" I asked. He didn't answer.

"Hey, Mike," I said, reaching over to touch his arm. He winced. That's when I noticed that he was bleeding. I motioned for everyone to stop.

"Mike, you're hit!" I said.

He stopped, looked at me, blood dripping from his arm, and collapsed to the ground.

Terror gripped me. *No, no, no, you can't die Mike!*

I opened his jacket. He was hit just below the shoulder.

"I'll be fine, kid. Just a little woozy," said Mike.

Daniel and Sophia came over. I opened Mike's backpack and found some bandages.

"He looks like he's lost a lot of blood," said Daniel.

Daniel and I wrapped him as best we could and put his jacket back on. *Please let him be alright,* I prayed.

"We're close to the farmhouse," I said. "Dmitry, we'll have to help him walk."

"I'll help," said Daniel and we lifted him to his feet. Then we each took an arm and placed it over our shoulders.

Another man stepped forward. It was the same man who had given Mike such a hard time about us before we left.

"Here, let me." He stepped in, took Mike's arm off my shoulder, and put it on his. "We need you to lead us." He smiled and nodded his head.

We made it to the edge of the woods. Misha and Natalia were waiting. Ahead of us was a field and beyond that the farmhouse. We were nearly there.

"Dmitry, scout along the tree line to the left for anything out of the ordinary. I don't want any surprises when we hit that field. Liza, you take my rifle and check to the right."

I went over to Mike who was leaning against a

tree.

"You doing good?" I asked. I handed him some water.

"Good, kid, I'm just fine. I can make it from here."

Dmitry and Liza came back and gave us the all clear.

"Here we go, folks. The last leg of our journey. Stick with us and stay together. We don't get off duty until you get to that farmhouse safe and sound."

We started walking across the field. Halfway across we saw someone dressed in farmer jeans and a plaid shirt walking and waving at us.

"Alex Krisko?" he yelled. I aimed my rifle in his direction.

Mike was right behind me with Daniel still supporting him.

"Mike, you know this guy?"

He tried to focus for a minute, then he smiled.

"That's Stas, your contact, kid. We made it."

When we got to the farmhouse, Stas introduced us to his wife, Victoria.

They had a table set up on the porch with food for everyone. It was a long porch, about knee high, with no railings. It ran the length of the farmhouse.

"Welcome." she smiled.

Stas saw Mike and took him inside to get patched up.

"Please, come and get something to eat," said Victoria.

Anton and I sat down on the edge of the porch.

"We did it, Alex. We got all these people to a safe place and got Daniel and Sophia back together again. I feel good."

"Me, too," I answered.

"Me, too, what?" asked Dmitry.

He, Liza, Natalia, and Misha walked up and stood in front of us.

"Feel good about the mission," said Anton.

They all smiled in agreement.

"You know what we need?" asked Anton. "A name!"

Just then Vika walked out of the house and

overheard. "Mike calls you the pains in his…"

"Nooo! That's a terrible name!" laughed Anton.

"Is Mike OK?" I asked Vika. *Please say yes.*

"He is. He's lost a lot of blood. As soon as we leave, I'm taking him to Dr. Holda."

"How about the Fighting Freaks for a name?" asked Misha.

"Or the Running Rascals," said Natalia.

"The Brave Boys and Two Girls." laughed Dmitry. Liza smacked him hard.

We were laughing and fooling around when someone behind me called,

"Alex, Anton?"

We turned around, and standing there with a big smile was Irina!

Anton and I sat there dumbstruck. I felt like I would black out. *I must be hallucinating,* I thought. I turned my back to her and closed my eyes as hard as I could.

When I opened them, I looked over at Anton, sitting there, speechless. I slowly turned and looked again. It *was* her! It was Irina!

I was overwhelmed with emotions, love, hate, resentment, relief, gratitude. I turned and ran to the barn. I opened the door and went inside. I paced like a madman. I needed to clear my thoughts.

I sat on a bale of hay that was against the wall across from the empty stalls. I held my head, trying to make sense of what was happening.

Why now? Why did she show up after all this time just when I had gotten myself, and Anton patched up and put back together?

The door opened. I didn't have to look up to know who it was. Irina walked over and sat next to me. She touched my hand. I pulled away as if burned by fire.

"We need to talk," she said.

"Maybe you need to talk. I don't. I can't think of one thing to say to you that would be kind, Irina."

Paul heard our exchange from the open doorway. He walked in and spoke to Irina.

"I know you want to talk to Alex alone, Irina, but I want to say something first." He looked over at me.

"Alex, I can understand that you're still pissed, but it's about time to let go, don't you think?"

"No! I don't think. She left us on our own at our

lowest point. She just walked out and never looked back. Now that we've survived without her and managed to do something for ourselves, she thinks she can just walk back into our lives?"

"Listen to yourself, man! She's not your mother!" snapped Paul.

The words stung like a slap in the face.

"She was a sixteen-year-old girl who was beaten by her father, put in a hospital, then told she was going to a place where she'd most likely be beaten again and again. She was scared to death." He walked over and put a hand on Irina's shoulder.

"So were we, Paul. So were we."

"And what on God's green earth did you expect her to do about it? She was a kid, too."

I looked at her. She was crying. She reminded me of Anna, a scared little girl looking for approval.

I saw Anton standing at the door, watching.

"You said you'd come back for us," I said to her. She just looked at me, tears running down her cheeks.

"She tried, man. When the riots started a year ago, she tried to leave Donetsk. When the guards at a checkpoint tried to stop her from leaving the city, she fought them, and she was arrested. My boss called in some favors, and we bought her way out of jail."

I just sat there, trying to digest what Paul was telling me.

Anton came over. "Alex? What do you want me to do?"

I looked at him, then back at Irina, still trying to sort out my feelings. Paul was right. What did I expect from her? She was barely a year older than I was.

I felt the hate and resentment fading away. What remained was love and forgiveness. I looked directly into Irina's eyes, as I said to Anton, "Hug your big sister hello. She's finally back with us, where she belongs."

She threw herself at Anton and me. We cried and laughed for what seemed like forever.

Paul came over and put his hand on my shoulder. I stood up, wiped my tears and held out my hand to him. He took it, pulled me in, and hugged me.

"What are you two doing here anyway?" I asked.

"Same thing you're doing. We work with the opposition. We're picking up your cargo!"

"I wonder if there's any food left," said Anton.

"You still a bottomless pit when it comes to food?" asked Irina.

"Is he! You see this empty field? It was full of corn and cabbage when we got here!" I joked.

"Yuk, yuk! Very funny," said Anton. I tousled his hair.

"Knock it off!" he said trying to smooth it back in place.

We got plates of food and sat back on the porch. We laughed, teased and joked. Dmitry, Liza, Natalia, and Misha told stories about Anton and me, so did Irina and Paul. We responded by telling our versions. One thing led to another and then it got physical. Dmitry pulled me down in a headlock. Anton jumped on top of Dmitry. Liza tickled Anton, soon Misha and Natalia joined in.

We were rolling, wrestling and laughing in the dirt. Paul and Irina looked at each other and dove right in the middle.

Mike walked out of the house with support from Vika. He was weak, but the bleeding had stopped. Vika helped him sit on a chair.

We stopped wrestling to say "hi."

Liza looked over at Dmitry and me, pointed, and

started laughing. When we looked back at her, we realized why. We were all covered in rich black dirt. We fell back laughing.

"Well, mission complete, Vika," said Mike. "They were as good as any soldiers I've ever served with. You'd never know by looking at them, but they're a hell of a group! They're gonna help us win this war."

"Hey, kid, Vika says you want a name. I've got a name for you," shouted Mike.

"What?" asked Anton.

"The Army of Orphans!"